Dom combed his fingers through Luci's hair and she closed her eyes against the need to lean into his touch....

"I'm as good as anyone on the team ever was," she said, and couldn't help the note of challenge in her voice. "I can do this." For the first time in a long while, the stir of something waking deep inside Luci fluttered alive. She'd loved the team. She'd loved saving lives. She'd loved knowing her special skill could make a difference. Or destroy her world.

Dom's smile canted up slowly, reaching all the way up to his eyes, making them glitter with humor that caused her to feel lighter. He slouched in that sexy way of his, compelling someone unaware of his lethal skill to believe they had nothing to fear from him. He deepened his drawl, letting its smoothness reverberate like a caress. "Then it's a date, darlin'."

SYLVIE KURTZ
PRIDE OF A HUNTER

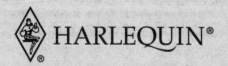

HARLEQUIN®

TORONTO • NEW YORK • LONDON
AMSTERDAM • PARIS • SYDNEY • HAMBURG
STOCKHOLM • ATHENS • TOKYO • MILAN • MADRID
PRAGUE • WARSAW • BUDAPEST • AUCKLAND

To Joyce—for the support and friendship.

A special thank-you to:
Mary Kennedy—for the forensic psychology help.
Chris Maddocks—for the sniper help.

ISBN 0-373-22872-4

PRIDE OF A HUNTER

ABOUT THE AUTHOR

Flying an eight-hour solo cross-country in a Piper Arrow with only the airplane's crackling radio and a large bag of M&M's for company, Sylvie Kurtz realized a pilot's life wasn't for her. The stories zooming in and out of her mind proved more entertaining than the flight itself. Not a quitter, she finished her pilot's course and earned her commercial license and instrument rating.

Since then, she has traded in her wings for a keyboard where she lets her imagination soar to create fictional adventures that explore the power of love and the thrill of suspense. When not writing, she enjoys the outdoors with her husband and two children, quilt-making, photography and reading whatever catches her interest.

You can write to Sylvie at P.O. Box 702, Milford, NH 03055. And visit her Web site at www.sylviekurtz.com.

Books by Sylvie Kurtz

CAST OF CHARACTERS

Lucinda Walden Taylor—All the sniper-turned-soccer-mom wanted was a quiet life for her and her son.

Dominic Skyralov—The Seeker knew Luci's deepest secrets.

Cole Taylor—Luci's husband; Dom's best friend. He was dead, but the memory of his death festered guilt in both Luci and Dom.

Brendan Taylor—The son Cole never knew existed and Luci desperately wanted to protect from a life of violence.

Warren Swanson—His goal was to expunge the sins of the soiled.

Laynie McDaniels—She was the first to die for her sins.

Jill Walden Courville—Luci's sister was Warren's latest pigeon.

Jeff Courville—The geeky boy reminded Warren of himself.

Joe Bob Grigsby—The escaped felon chose to kill rather than surrender.

Amber Fitzgerald—The fitness instructor softened the prey.

Prologue

In the hours between three and five in the morning, life slowed to a crawl. Her body's need for sleep had Lucinda Walden fighting to keep her eyes open. She pulled her eye off-scope to blink out the fatigue, then resettled her right shoulder over the rubber butt pad of her rifle. Eye on-scope again, she panned left to right, across the door and windows of the two-story shack in the middle of nowhere in North Texas, checking for activity.

Her job was simple—be ready to kill, but avoid shooting at all cost. Discipline. Control. Restraint.

Sweltering heat, even so early on this August morning, had sweat streaming down her sides, sticking every stitch of camouflage clothing to her skin. Fog, graying everything in its path and rising in tongues off the pond beside the house, gave the run-down place the look of hell.

"Sierra One to TOC," Luci whispered into the mic resting against her jaw to the Tactical Operations Center. The hostage taker couldn't hear her, but he was so close in her scope that it seemed as if he should. "I have subject movement. White alpha three." Back side of the house, first floor, third window. "White male, five foot ten, one hundred and sixty pounds, dark hair and beard. Bare torso, low-slung jeans. Two pistols stuffed down his pants. One rifle cruising for a target. He has the kid on his hip." Their subject looked like a desperado in a really bad Western.

"Copy, Sierra One."

Luci tried shutting her mind off to the bawling four-year-old the hostage taker had strapped to his waist like a lifesaver, but couldn't keep the shine of his tears from invading. *Don't you worry, little one. We'll get you out safe. That's what this team does. We save lives.*

Hostage negotiations boiled down to building rapport, calming fears and making consequences acceptable. But talking sometimes wasn't the solution. This hostage taker wasn't in the mood for rapport. The instinct to save his own sorry hide was putting two innocents at risk. And with three consecutive life sentences to serve, he had nothing left to lose.

The Special Operations Group was twenty-six hours into a situation with the escaped felon. He'd taken his ex-girlfriend and her four-year-old boy as live body armor to buy his freedom once the deputy marshals tasked with bringing him back to prison had cornered him.

Luci was five hours into her second six-hour shift with only snakes, spiders and scorpions for company as she lay in the tall grass on the hill overlooking the house.

And Joe Bob Grigsby, the piece of garbage who'd started the whole thing by flying his coop, had thrown the phone out the window half an hour ago and traded it for a shot of something that had him wired and his hostages blubbering in utter terror.

This couldn't go on much longer. If Dom couldn't talk this guy down, then no one could. Which would rev up the assault team. Cole had to be chomping at the bit to knock down the door and kick some butt.

Dom and Cole. The mule and the thoroughbred. Each excellent at his job. Each as opposite as black and white. Each the best of friends. One was her confidant, the other her lover. No, make that her brand-new husband—though no one else on the team knew. The thought of her elopement brought a small smile to her lips. She and Cole and Dom had all competed and bonded in the same training class and, although like tended to mix with like, their odd circle of friendship had endured.

Together, they worked magic.

She'd punched holes through thousands of targets, but because of Dom's smooth-talking ways and Cole's take-no-prisoners daring, she'd never had to make that split-second decision to plug a bullet through anyone's brain stem and end a life. Knock on wood, so far, all of their operations had ended without a shot fired.

"TOC to all units, stand by to copy." The voice of the Special Operations Group leader boomed through Luci's earpiece. Something was up. A shot of adrenaline spiked through her veins, brightening the crown of sun spearing through the fog.

"Sierra One, ready to copy." The other units, assault and sniper, keyed in.

Her father had once told her that a pilot's life was long hours of boredom punctuated by seconds of sheer terror. A sniper's life wasn't much different. Hurry up and wait. The U.S. Marshals Service hadn't promised her glamour, but they had promised her a chance to prove herself. Four years ago, that had seemed like more than she'd gotten out of life so far.

Twenty-six hours of trying to end a situation peaceably had come down to the next few seconds.

One second. One shot. No second chances. A miss meant a failure. A hit, two lives saved. *Are you ready, Luci? Can you do it? Can you take a life? Can you finally prove you're good enough?*

She centered the crosshairs in the scope tube. Her index finger rested on the trigger guard. She looked into the living room, one hundred and ninety yards away, with an intimacy that was deceiving. Joe Bob hadn't shaved since he'd run. The five o'clock shadow had grown into a short beard. His skin was oily with sweat. His brown eyes were wild and the whites spidered with red. She could almost smell the sourness of his body, the alcohol on his breath, the desperation in his rage-spiked pulse.

"Hotel One to TOC. We're at Yellow." The assault team had reached the forward rallying point, the last position of cover and concealment.

"Copy, Hotel One. I have you at Yellow."

Luci aligned her body with the recoil path, pressed her hip against the ground and spread her knees for stability. *Slow and easy.*

She raised the elevation to compensate for the high humidity. With air this still, she didn't have to accommodate for windage. The crosshairs in her scope fluxed slightly as a wake of adrenaline flowed out of her muscles. She settled back on Joe Bob's face.

The assault team waited for the order to breach.

"TOC to all units. You have compromise authority and permission to move to Green."

The group leader counted down the launch sequence. "Three…"

The world blackened and narrowed to that third window on the first floor. To Joe Bob's crazed face as he buzzed back and forth across the window, brandishing the petrified child like a sack of feed. *Just a few more seconds, baby, and we'll have you out and safe.*

"Two…"

Concentrate. Calm yourself. Slow the heartbeat. Her heart pumped with a trained rhythm that fed her brain oxygen but didn't interfere with her shot. She settled the crosshairs on the tip of Joe Bob's nose.

"One…"

Then came the pause that seemed to hang in the air forever before the world exploded into action. The assault team, clad in black, blew down the door—no flash-bang devices because of the kid—and raced in. Every move was a well-practiced choreography. *"Drop the gun! Drop the gun!"*

The woman screamed. The child howled.

Joe Bob stopped his mad pacing. He dropped the rifle and stuck a pistol under the boy's chin.

Luci sucked in air and eased it out.

Committed, she increased pressure on the trigger.

The world shattered, spewing chaos into the air like Fourth of July fireworks.

Her ears rang.

Bodies dropped.

And the ground ran red with blood.

Chapter One

Seven years later

His mind seventeen miles away from where he sat in the basement bunker of the Aerie in Wintergreen, New Hampshire, Dominic Skyralov paid little attention to the morning briefing as he carved a bite out of the almond coffee cake on his plate and washed it down with warm green tea.

"That's all, gentlemen." Sebastian Falconer, head of Seekers, Inc., closed the top file in front of him. The briefing was ending, and Dom wasn't quite sure how to bring up the subject of his quandary. "Check your PDAs for updates."

Dom pulled what was left of the almond coffee cake on the platter toward him. "I need a word with you."

Falconer nodded and leaned back into his chair, the picture of patience.

Sabriel Mercer, dark and brooding, peeled himself off the shadows of the wall and left without a word. Nothing new there. Dom often wondered what had scarred the man so deeply he couldn't trust himself to speak.

Noah Kingsley halted his swift unplugging of snakes of wires attached to his various computer accessories. Looking from one man to the other, he snapped his red suspenders and said, "I'll get his later."

Hale Harper, usual glower in place, gathered his notes. "Hang on, Kingsley. I need some information from you."

"Follow me to my parlor." Kingsley waggled his eyebrows.

Liv, Falconer's wife, poked her head through the door, blocking their escape. Her short chocolate-brown hair looked wind-tousled and her blue eyes gleamed with mischief. "All done?"

Falconer's whole body relaxed as if he'd inhaled a powerful tranquilizer and a smile invaded his stern face. When it came to his wife, their fierce leader was a push-over. "All done. Coming in?"

"Um, no. I need to borrow Gray."

"Me?" Grayson Reed halted midstride on the far side of the room as if he'd been frozen by a photographer's flash.

"Uh-oh," Kingsley teased as he slipped by Liv. "You're in trouble now."

"You're getting married in a month," Liv said, displaying a neat row of white teeth.

"I am." A goofy grin took over Reed's toothpaste-commercial smile and warmth flooded the silver steel of his eyes. Even the sideways mention of his fiancée, Abbie, turned Hollywood veneer into soap star mush. "Oh, God, I am."

Harper exaggerated a shiver. "Man, I feel for you. I'd rather face a felon in a dark alley than sit through the torture of picking out china patterns."

Dom couldn't help the tickle of envy at Reed's happiness. He'd imagined he'd have himself a team of rug rats by now. That's what happened when someone stole your heart and didn't give it back. You found yourself alone, wanting what you couldn't have. Especially now, when he was about to reopen a wound best left alone.

"Weddings don't plan themselves, you know." Liv grabbed the stunned Reed's shirtsleeve and pulled him into the hall. "We have a lot to do and not much time. Abbie's upstairs, waiting. How do you feel about pumpkin and cranberry?"

"Um, they make good pies?"

"Color schemes, you silly man." Liv's laughter faded as she and Reed climbed the stone stairs up to Liv's sunny office.

Once Liv disappeared, Falconer swiveled his black leather chair to face Dom. "What's on your mind?"

"I found our target." For the past six months, Dom had been tracking down a hit-and-run groom. The scam was swift and efficient, leaving heartache and ruin in its wake. The guy wooed divorcées, married them, drained them of all assets, then disappeared, taking on another identity and starting all over again somewhere else. His marks didn't even know they'd been hit until it was too late.

After the con artist's last foray, the bride, Laynie McDaniels, distraught by her losses, hanged herself in a motel room closet. She'd spent the past seven months on life support and had recently died. Her parents, Austin high society, feeling the authorities weren't doing enough to capture and punish their daughter's tormentor, had hired Seekers, Inc. a month after Laynie's accident to locate the "dirty, rotten scoundrel" and bring him to justice. Circumstances pointed to foul play, but he needed court-solid evidence to back up the gut feeling. "He's going by Warren Swanson this time. He's passing himself off as a private detective in Nashua. And he's about to strike again."

"Let's make sure we stop him before he does."

"We need irrefutable evidence."

"Uh-uh."

Dom shoveled coffee cake into his mouth and chewed, trying to stay ahead of his bleak thoughts. Sweetheart scams rarely got prosecuted because who was to say that all hadn't been given for love and the angry spurned lover hadn't simply regretted her generosity? Not that many people reported the crime in the first place. Who wanted to admit they had been duped by a lover? The con artist counted on the character flaw of pride to get away and live to perpetuate the scam on some other unsuspecting love-starved pigeon.

Catching this guy would mean riding a delicate balance between putting an innocent woman in danger and making sure they got enough to put the guy behind bars for a good long time. Dom had to make this stop the impostor's last. Evidence wasn't a problem. Dom already had a six-inch-thick file with a number of aliases and addresses. What he lacked was proof of criminal intent. "I have a plan."

"Shoot."

The plan was simple enough: slip into Marston's tightly knit community and pose as Luci Taylor's boyfriend. Once he was close to both victim and con man, he could gather evidence. Dom reached for the mug of tea and drained it as if it were a shot of whiskey. Going in with guns blazing wasn't going to work with this guy. He was too good at disappearing and reinventing himself. Dom couldn't risk losing him again. This cover was the best way to snag him. "It requires going undercover to catch him hand in the cookie jar. I need to get close to him, win his trust."

"I don't have a problem with that."

Nope, nothing out of the ordinary. Just a run-of-the-mill operation.

Except for one thing.

"The victim is Jillian Courville." Dom chewed on the last piece of coffee cake and almost choked on it as it went down crooked.

"Is that a problem?"

Dom stared at the crumbs on his plate and swirled the fork through them. "Jill is Luci Taylor's younger sister." Jill was a spoiled divorcée who'd made out rich in her divorce settlement. And Luci? Falconer already knew about the Hostage Rescue Team and the way Cole Taylor had died. Dom looked around for more coffee cake and realized he'd eaten the whole thing without tasting it.

"Ah." Hands tented over his lap, chin resting on his upraised fingers, Falconer rocked his chair back and forth. "I can send someone else."

"No, I've got this guy's number." Dom had seen the havoc the con man had wreaked. Cuffing him was personal by now.

"What's the problem then?"

"Luci." Dom would be a reminder of everything she'd left behind, of everything she'd lost. He'd watched her for the past few days. Her routine was her comfort—the mornings spent in her fields, the afternoons in her barn, the mad rush of late afternoons taken up by her son's needs. The master sniper had turned herself into the picture of a suburban soccer mom. She wouldn't appreciate him showing up on her front steps.

But making peace and putting criminals behind bars where they could hurt only themselves had been his mission since his seventeen-year-old brother had been killed by a small-time con man. He couldn't stop now just because his pride might get dinged. "She's not going to like having anyone mess with her piece of paradise."

"She doesn't have to know."

He'd thought of that, but once he put the plan through its paces, he figured trying to get one past Luci would bring more conflict than it would resolve. She might think she'd left her sniper days behind, but her warrior's instincts were as sharp as ever. Twice, she'd nearly caught him following her as he'd tried to establish Jill's habit pattern. "I need her help to get close to Swanson so he doesn't feel threatened."

"You can't have it both ways."

Dom pushed away the plate. "I know."

"What can I do to help?"

"I need cover. He's bound to check me out and it looks like he can do it, too, since he's got Jill's numbers all lined up. Leave the football history there for common ground. Swanson's sporting a Super Bowl ring. Not his, mind you, just part of his cover. A salesman, maybe. That wouldn't be a threat to him, especially if I'm not so good at it."

Falconer's grin slid sideways. "That's going to be hard to do. You could sell manure to a pig farmer."

"Aw, shucks, Falconer, I'm just a redneck from down Brazos County way. I couldn't sell a plug nickel to a leaking dam."

Falconer chuckled. "I'll have Kingsley fix you up."

"I'll need data support."

"You've got it." Falconer gathered up his files. "Anything else?"

How about a face Luci wouldn't hate on sight? "I've got everything covered."

Everything but his dumb heart, and he couldn't let Luci know she still had it in her back pocket. Not if he wanted her help.

"Brendan!" Luci Taylor bowled through the creaking back door of her Victorian fixer-upper, walked out of her garden clogs and into the kitchen without breaking stride. The room was a chaos of half-finished jobs, but she didn't have time to worry about the cupboard doors waiting refinishing in the barn or the last wall of wallpaper waiting to be stripped. "We're going to be late for soccer practice."

"I can't find my shoes." The small voice came from somewhere in the front. She suspected the living room where her six-year-old son had surely parked his butt before the forbidden television. Her five minutes of picking basil leaves had turned into an hour of weeding, and he'd taken advantage of her distractibility.

Luci stuck her hands under running water and washed off the rich garden dirt with a homemade cake of rosemary soap. "They'll be much easier to find once you turn off the TV."

"Aww, Mo-om."

"Come on. We have to pick up Jeff." Jill's carnival committee meeting was running late—as usual. On the positive side, if Jill hadn't called requesting a ride for her seven-year-old son, Brendan might have missed practice altogether. Again. Luci still had summer's unstructured time on her mind and, one week into school, she hadn't quite gotten into the fall routine yet. She had to learn to wear a watch and not let time get away from her. Other moms managed to keep a regular schedule. She should be able to also.

"Do we hafta? He's such a baby."

Like a six-year-old was all grown-up. Luci transferred the cell phone from her sweatshirt pocket to her purse, then collected the storage bag of oranges she'd quartered earlier from the fridge. "He's your cousin and you're to be nice to him."

"He's a dork."

"A dork who fixes your computer games." That Jeff wasn't athletic wasn't his fault. His talents had a more intellectual bent—something she'd wished for her own son. To her utter devastation, Brendan had inherited his father's craving for risk. She'd spent enough time at the local emergency room to be on a first-name basis with both first-shift and second-shift personnel.

Luci strode into the living room, flicked off the television and urged her son off his nest of plush pillows and toward the kitchen. Maggie, the brown-and-blond mutt seemingly put together from spare parts, jumped off the couch with a guilty look and slunk into the kitchen, wagging her tail warily. Luci didn't have time to care about dog hair, so ignoring the transgression seemed best for her sanity at the moment. "Come on, Brendan. Your shoes are by the door where they belong."

"Can we stop at the playground on the way home?"

"Not today." Luci ruffled her son's shock of dark hair.

"How come?"

"We don't have time. I have a batch of pesto to get ready for the country club restaurant by tomorrow morning." Not to mention the herb logs or the herb vinaigrette. And that didn't take into consideration the gardens that needed cleaning up or the goats that needed feeding and milking on a regular basis. She loved all of it, really she did. She just needed a few more hours every day to make it all work out.

"Aww, Mo-om."

"Aww, Bren-dan." She grabbed her purse and the bag of orange sections. The dog danced all around her, wound up by the buzz of energy Brendan and their lateness created. Surveying her son, she noted the shin pads loosely cuffed around his lower legs and mouth guard dangling from a finger. "Do you have water?"

Brendan lifted his Nalgene bottle from the deacon's bench by the door. "And my ball." He scooped the black-and-white ball out from under the bench with his sock-clad foot.

"Let's go." She slipped on a pair of felt clogs, grabbed the cleats, opened the back door and shooed out the dog.

Just as Brendan maneuvered the ball out the back door, the strangled sound of the bell on the front door rang. *Not now.* She snagged her van keys from the horseshoe-shaped holder by the door. "Get in the van and wait for me. Don't touch anything. And we're not taking Maggie, so don't let her in."

As Luci pounded to the door, she juggled everything in her arms to free a hand. She opened the door, ready to put her ill-timed visitor off. Whatever word had meant to cross her lips remained locked in her voice box.

"Hi, Luce. Can I come in?"

The sight of Dominic Skyralov, big as life and broad as a bull, knocked her back two steps and seven years. His blond hair had darkened to caramel. But otherwise, nothing much had changed about the smooth-talking cowboy. His blue eyes still matched the well-washed denim of his skin-hugging jeans, still could read right through her, still made her want to confess her deepest sins. He'd been her best friend for four years. Then everything had changed. Now the sight of him called back her darkest memories and the nauseating disorientation that came with them.

"No." She hung on to the brass doorknob as if it could save her from the flood of pain that rushed through her. "You can't come in."

"I need to talk to you."

"I'm sorry." She shook her head, trying desperately to break apart the image of blood, of horror, of Cole dead on the floor, of red staining the dirty boards of that bleak North Texas shack. "I'm on my way out."

Dom nodded. A good-old-boy gesture that was as part of him as his inbred politeness. "I'll come back, then. When would be good for you?"

Never. Her ears rang. Her vision narrowed and blackened. *Oh, God, no.* Him coming back would make this even worse. She'd have all the time in between to re-live her worst nightmare over and over again. Cole falling, bleeding, dying. Closing her eyes, she swallowed hard. "Say whatever you have to say and leave. I'm in a hurry."

"It's a nice place you've got here."

"No, Dom, don't." Her voice strained between clenched teeth. "I know how you work. Put your subject at ease, then slip in the punch. Just get to the point, okay?" She couldn't take his smooth negotiator's voice, that slow Texas drawl, chipping away at her calm until he found her soft spot and bored in for the kill.

"There's a con man in town. He marries divorcées and bleeds them dry. I need you to help me gather evidence and provide me with some cover."

Why don't you just take a knife and twist it in my guts? "You are *not* bringing trouble here. Do you hear? You are *not* bringing trouble to this family. You are *not* bringing trouble to this community."

"He's engaged to your sister."

The soft punch of his words knocked her breathless. "Now I know you're lying. My sister isn't seeing any-one."

Then Luci remembered Jill's bubblier-than-usual voice this morning as she'd issued a dinner invitation for Saturday and added she had a surprise. Luci had assumed Jill had scraped up another blind date to force on her. *Jilly, what have you done?* "I'm leaving now. And when I get back, I don't want to see you or your truck in my driveway. Is that understood?"

Another nod. But he wasn't moving. He wasn't leaving. His big body became an iceberg she feared wouldn't melt away until he'd done what he'd set out to accomplish. "Thing is, Luce, whether you want it or not, trouble's here and it's not me. The last woman this con man married died. You don't want that for Jill. As much as you two rub each other raw, you love her."

He shrugged as if he weren't ripping the world she'd worked so hard to create to shreds, as if he didn't have a care in the world. But he did. Dom had always cared too much. That's why she couldn't bear the sight of him. "You want to see trouble go away, Luce. You want your neat little life to go on. Then you need my help."

Shaking her head, she snorted. That was just like him, turning this whole thing on her, making it her fault, her failure. She didn't need this. She was already serving her time in hell. She was doing her penance. She deserved her small corner of peace and security. And even if she didn't, Brendan did.

"I'll take care of Jill myself. Goodbye." Heart pounding, tears clawing up her throat, she slammed the door in Dom's face and ran out the back door to the minivan where her son waited unaware that a monster worse than any video game's had just invaded their bright little world.

Chapter Two

The horror Dom had resurrected by his presence clung to Luci's skin like a disease and had her even more distracted than usual. At every stop sign, at every red light, her mind conjured up images that flowed and mutated in nightmarelike exaggeration from Cole's dead body, lying in that forsaken shack in Texas seven years ago, to the possibility of Jill's body, lying in a pool of blood in her own home. How could Dom do this to her? He knew her secret, had to know it still ate at her and always would, no matter how far she'd run from it.

Her family was all she had. She couldn't let anything happen to them. And the last thing she needed was Dom there in Marston reminding her of her guilt.

By the time Luci reached the recreation fields on Depot Road, the lot was filled and she had to squeeze her minivan in a slot that was too small. To make things even more stressful, practice turned out to be a game and Howie Dunlap, the coach, wasn't too happy that Brendan, his star player, was late. Luci refrained from pointing out he was lucky they'd showed up in the right place.

Entreating Jeff to come out of the van and put on his

cleats took another ten minutes of trying patience. The boy wasn't an athlete and knew it. He played soccer only to please his mother and spend time with Brendan, whom he adored. And although Brendan often complained about his cousin's klutziness, he always included him in whatever game they played and bopped anyone who tried to make fun of him. Not Luci's favorite manner of conflict resolution, but explaining why this method was the last resort fell short of logical to Brendan when it solved his problem so neatly.

The moms were already gathered along the sideline, the brisk breeze barely moving their styled locks. They sat in a row, roosting and clucking, on their folding red canvas chairs like brooding hens. Only Luci's blue chair stood out. She didn't see the point of buying a new color chair every time Brendan graduated teams.

"Late again, Luci." Sally Kennison, in her perfectly pleated trousers and polished loafers, looked down her long nose as Luci struggled to free the chair from its carrying case. "You really ought to treat yourself to a watch."

"Goats don't run by a clock." Luci had to let pop out the one wrong thing to remind the country club set that she was an outsider who worked a lowly farm for a living. Hard to believe she'd once had iron control over every cell of her body. But August always shook her up and shredded her focus. Getting back in sync took more time every year.

Sally's perfectly manicured nails waived down the sideline. "Yes, well, you obviously aren't late because you took the time to clean up. Sit downwind, please." A few of the other moms sniggered and the gossip

turned back to who was doing what to whom. Luci
tuned them out and focused on the kids.

On the field, two teams of six- and seven-year-olds
mobbed the ball and somehow moved it up and down
the field. Pacing each of the sidelines, the two coaches
barked suggestions that were mostly ignored as the kids
concentrated on kicking the black-and-white ball toward the goal.

At halftime, Luci distributed the orange slices and
the kids turned them into orange-peel smiles.

That's when Jill showed up, hurrying in high-heel-
induced ministeps toward the field. As Luci watched her
baby sister, Dom's voice came back to haunt her.

*There's a con man in town. He marries divorcées and
bleeds them dry.*

The last woman this con man married died.

He's engaged to your sister.

Jill couldn't take another heartache. Not after the
way John Jeffery Courville the Second had left her for
an older woman. She was just now rebounding from the
messy divorce.

Jill had the pert and sassy disposition of someone
who would appear young even when she was gray and
wrinkled. Her hazel eyes tilted up and crinkled at the
corners as if she were always smiling—even when she
cried. Her blond-highlighted brown hair was cut in a
bob she styled up or down, depending on her mood.
Today, she'd had the carnival committee meeting, so
she'd gone for the messy bun look—half intellectual,
but still showing she could have fun. Her beige linen
pants were too light, her strappy heels too high for soccer field sidelines, yet somehow, Jill pulled off the look

and fit in more with the Marston mommy-crowd than Luci did with her jeans and sweatshirt.

One of life's little jokes.

Jill fit in without trying; Luci never could, no matter how hard she tried. She should just stop caring, but somehow she couldn't.

She'd robbed Brendan of his father. She'd do everything she could so Brendan could have as normal a childhood as possible. She'd come back to Marston because her sister and her parents lived there. She'd grown up there. She felt safe there, even living on the periphery. And she wanted this safe, secure, small-town life with roots and family and community for Brendan. She wanted to raise her son out of the shadow of violence that tainted her past and had stolen part of his future.

"Who's winning?" Jill asked, plopping down her red chair, which opened for her as easily as an umbrella.

"It's a tie. One each."

"Oh, that's good."

"How was the carnival committee meeting?"

Jill cringed and shook her head. "Who would have thought that putting on a one-day fund-raising event at an elementary school would take such sharp negotiating skills? If we pull this off by next weekend, we'll be lucky."

Luci hooked an ankle over a knee, going for the relaxed look. "Hey, so I hear you have a new boyfriend."

Jill snapped up straight. "Who told you that?"

Shrugging, Luci pretended rapt attention at the game. "Sally Kennison." A small lie, but one Jill would believe. Everyone knew that Sally Kennison somehow funneled every scrap of gossip in town and dispersed it as freely as dandelion seeds.

"How could she possibly know?" Jill asked, narrowing her gaze at the woman in question, who was too busy gossiping to notice the deadly look spearing her.

"So, are you?" Luci asked, keeping an eye on Brendan's forward rush and her peripheral vision on Jill. Luci might have lost proficiency with a weapon, but other skills remained.

Jill stuck out her bottom lip. "Well, there goes my surprise."

"I thought your surprise was another blind date for me."

Jill snorted in an unladylike manner. "The world doesn't revolve around you, Luci."

"Tell me about it." Lately her world had seemed to spin totally out of control. And Dom's arrival, with his warnings of doom and gloom, certainly did nothing to slow down the crazy tilting. "So, who is he?"

Jill's face transformed into pure sunshine. "Oh, he's the most wonderful guy."

"Where'd you meet him?"

Jill giggled, making her look twelve. "It was such a coincidence. I met him at the club." Meaning the Marston Country Club on Flint Bridge Road, where all the who's who went to be seen. The only time anyone saw Luci there was when she delivered her organic vegetables, herbs and sauces—at the rear entrance, of course. "He was meeting a client for lunch and we literally ran into each other."

A five-alarm warning jangled in Luci's head. *Oh, Jilly, how could you fall for the oldest trick in the book?* "How long ago was that?"

Jill cheered Jeff on, even though he was just standing on the field, pushing up his glasses and watching the ball roll by. "A couple of weeks ago."

"So, tell me more." Luci kept her voice light, curious and panic free, even though the panic was digging needles in her chest.

"He's a dream. A real gentleman. He's a private investigator. Isn't that just so fascinating? You should see his office. It's right on Main Street in Nashua, and he has it fixed up like a movie set."

The better to play you with, Jilly. What was she going to do? If she tried telling Jill she was being conned, Jill would simply turn on her and accuse Luci of jealousy. "So I get to meet him tomorrow?"

"Yes. Mom and Dad'll be there, too."

Great, just what Luci needed—more criticism.

"Warren's going to grill some hamburgers for the kids, then he'll make some salmon steaks for the adults."

Oh, no, he was using downright dirty tactics to worm his way into Jill's heart. A man who could cook. Jill's soft spot. He was showing her he could take care of her every need. "Can I bring anything?"

Jill's nose wrinkled up in a cute, sassy way, as if she'd expected Luci's offer all along. "How about one of your apple tortes? Warren loves apples."

Luci cleared her throat at the sickening display of gush. With any luck, Warren's next apple pie would come courtesy of the corrections system. "Okay, sure."

Brendan kicked the ball straight at his cousin, giving him a chance to get into the play.

Jeff aimed his foot at the ball, managed to clip it with the side of his cleat and fell down hard on his backside.

The referee blew the whistle. The coach trotted onto the field and helped Jeff up. The crowd clapped. Once on the sideline, Jeff made a beeline for his mother.

"I fell down." Jeff sniffled and held up his arms. Jill, who'd jumped up when Jeff fell, crouched down to his eye level and let her son wrap his grubby arms around her pale pink cashmere sweater.

"I saw that."

"Brendan passed the ball to me, and—" Jeff hiccuped.

"And I saw you kick it right back to him. That was a good play. Way to be a team player!"

Jeff pulled away from Jill, smearing dirt on the collar of her sweater, and beamed. "Yeah. I made a play."

Jill pulled a handkerchief from her purse and dabbed at Jeff's grass-stained knee. "You're having fun, right?"

He nodded. Jill kissed his cheek, leaving behind the red imprint of her lipstick. "Well, that's all that matters."

She patted his bottom and urged him back toward his team.

"So what else do you know about this guy?" Luci asked and tried very hard to sound as if the answer didn't matter. "What's his name again? I mean, it seems like he came out of nowhere."

"It wasn't nowhere." Soiled handkerchief held between two fingers, Jill swiveled her head looking for a place to dispose of the offending square of material. "I told you. I met Warren at the club. I ran into him when I was late for a meeting, then Amber Fitzgerald introduced us. You know her. She runs the fitness center on Marketplace Road."

"Amber isn't exactly known for her stellar taste." She reminded Luci of a little drab brown mouse.

Jill pinched her lips, as if she were holding back a comment, then said, "Warren moved here last month from Florida, if you must know. The last hurricane tore down his office and he decided to move up north instead of rebuilding."

"He might regret that come January," Luci muttered. More likely he wouldn't even be here, if Dom was right. He'd be long gone with all of Jill's assets. God, Luci didn't want Dom to be right. How would Jill support her son? How would she get over another betrayal? Luci wanted everything to stay as it was, even if it meant she'd always be banned from the country club dining room and sniggered at by the other moms. At least everyone she loved would remain safe.

"Well, that's why we have airplanes," Jill said. "We can vacation somewhere warm."

Already Jill saw herself and Warren as a couple. Not good. The guy was moving fast. Another sign of a con man. Dazzle and disappear before the stars in the mark's eyes faded and she quite knew what had happened to her.

Jill stalked to the green garbage barrel by the parking lot and dumped her linen handkerchief.

That's when Luci noticed the truck. Big, bold and Aggie burgundy. Obviously, her days as a sniper hyperaware of her surroundings were long gone if she'd managed to miss a truck like that following her.

Luci tried her best to ignore Dom and his truck with its smoked glass, but her gaze kept drifting to the parking lot. Every sight of him would remind her of danger, of death, of everything she thought she'd left behind after Cole had died. Risk was no longer part of the equation of her life. She didn't want it back.

But there was no point pretending Warren hadn't already established a toehold in Jill's life. The trick was making sure he didn't get the rest of the foot in. She still had a few contacts. She'd verify what Dom had told her and make sure Jill wasn't hurt.

"I know how much J.J. hurt you when he left," Luci said once Jill had returned. "You wouldn't mind if I ran a background check on Warren, would you?"

"Oh, no." Jill shook a finger at her. "You are going to leave Warren alone. He's a good man, and I don't want you ruining this for me. What is it with you anyway? Why can't you ever be happy for me?"

"Of course I'm happy for you, Jill. But you're my little sister, and I don't want to see you hurt again."

"Warren would never hurt me." Jill's face turned soft and besotted again. "He cares for me. He takes care of me. He gave me this."

Jill plucked a small gold chain from under her sweater. A thumbnail-size diamond glittered in the afternoon sun, nearly blinding Luci with its brilliance. "He says it reminds him of my smile."

Cubic zirconium, no doubt. "It's, um, pretty."

"It's beautiful, and I'd love it even if it was paste."

Oh, God, Jill was in deep already. Warren was giving her gifts, gaining her confidence. How soon before he started asking her for money?

Jill lifted her chin and wrinkled her nose in that cute way she did when she was trying to hold back a smile. "Did you know you should check your credit report every year? You know, in case someone has bad information or is trying to steal your identity."

"Really?" *No, no, no, Jilly, you didn't fall for that,*

did you? Now he has all your financial information at his fingertips. The better to rob you blind with.

"Yes, and everything's just fine."

Of course it was. If it wasn't, Warren would have moved on to fatter prey. Luci glanced at Dom's truck and cursed him for plopping this mess in her lap.

Jill craned her neck in the direction of Luci's preoccupation. "Who's that?"

"Who's who?"

"The guy in the burgundy truck."

"An old friend." Luci had given up hunting a long time ago. But she couldn't just stand by and watch her sister be used and tossed aside. She had to do *something.* "He came to town unexpectedly."

"What kind of old friend?"

"Just a friend, Jill." At her sister's pout, Luci softened her tone. "Can I bring him to dinner on Saturday?"

Jill smirked. "But of course, Lucinda Louise. It's about time you found yourself a boyfriend."

"He's not a boyfriend. Just a friend."

"Sure, sure. Whatever you say. Bring him." From the middle of the field a whistle shrilled and a thunder of cheers rose. "Looks like the game's over. Meet you at The Leaning Pizza?"

"Can you take Brendan for me? I'll meet you later."

"Sure, take your time." Jill glanced at Dom's truck and slanted Luci a knowing smile. "If you're not there by the time we're ready to leave, I'll just take Brendan home with us."

"That won't be necessary."

Jill brushed at the dog hair decorating the front of Luci's sweatshirt. "Luci, you have to loosen up a bit."

Luci pantomimed a stringless puppet. "I'm so loose I can't keep track of time."

"Not that kind of loose." Jill tilted her head to one side, meeting Luci's gaze. "You need friends. You need fun. You need—" she leaned forward, cupped a hand around her mouth and whispered "—*sex*."

The sizzling sound of the word kicked Luci's midriff with an almost forgotten punch. "*That* is not the answer to everything."

Especially not with Dom. He knew too much about her. He'd seen the black mark on her soul. He'd once been a friend. But he could never be a lover. And Luci certainly hoped Jill's relationship with Warren The Worm hadn't progressed to that intimate stage.

Jill waggled her eyebrows. "But it sure makes everything rosy."

Luci barely managed to swallow her groan. So much for that hope. Warren had obviously wowed Jill in bed, too.

Jeff and Brendan pounded their way toward their parent. Each grabbed one of Jill's hands and started dragging her toward her Lexus SUV. "Come on, Mom."

"Come on, Auntie Jill. It's pizza time!" The DVD player was the big pull for Brendan wanting to ride with his aunt to the post-game party.

Jill pretended helpless worry at her captors' strength. Head thrown back, laughing, she let the boys lead her away. "Guess I'd better go. Take your time."

"Come on, Mom," Brendan called over his shoulder.

"I'll be there in a bit. Be good for Aunt Jill."

Jill's retort was lost in the confusion of little boy rambunctiousness.

Dragging her uncooperative folding chair behind her, Luci reluctantly made her way to Dom's truck at the edge of the now near empty parking lot and rapped her knuckles against the passenger's side window. The tinted glass wound down silently and smoothly.

Her heart rate doubled as his face appeared. The soft blue of his eyes was filled with compassion, as if he truly understood the depth of the wound on her soul and the toll his presence was taking on her. He'd loved Cole, too, and Cole was the one thing they could never discuss if they were to make it through until Jill's predator was behind bars. "We need to talk."

DOM REACHED ACROSS the truck's cab for the passenger door handle, but Luci clamped a hand around the door and held it firmly in place. She stood there, not saying anything, the wide yawn of the years gaping black and empty between them, a burned-out territory neither of them wanted to revisit. Too much guilt. Too much regret. Too much helplessness.

"Luci—"

"Show me everything you have on this guy who's preying on Jill." Luci's green eyes were scowling slits. Spikes of ripe wheat hair stuck out from the long braid twisting over her shoulder. He couldn't decide if the redness of her cheeks was due to the coolness of the breeze or the heat of her anger.

"Most of my files are back at the office."

"Talk then. That's your specialty, isn't it?"

The negotiator was always the man in the middle, and that seemed to have been Dom's position from Day One. He was the middle child, the go-between for his parents and his brothers. The third wheel between Luci and Cole.

And now he was the outsider who was coming between two sisters.

"I'll talk, Luce. Question is, are you ready to listen?"

Her lips tightened into a straight, hard line. "He conned Jill into giving him the information he needed to run a credit check on her."

Dom didn't like seeing a thin shell of the bright, vibrant woman he'd once known. "He's moving faster than usual."

Swanson had already gained his mark's confidence and was stepping up to the next stage. Soon he'd start asking for money. A bit here to tide him over while he waited for a check to come in. A bit there while he waited for a client to pay a bill. And Jill, flush with the soft and fuzzy blanket of new love, would gladly fork it over.

"Usual?" Luci asked, frowning as if she had a headache. "How many times has he done this?"

"I've managed to track down four. Jill is number five."

Luci closed her eyes and swallowed hard. How much was it costing her to hold herself together? The years had deepened the lines of sorrow around her eyes, but hadn't diminished her beauty. Something about the softness of her features, the fullness of her lips, the grounding green of her eyes made him want to sigh, snuggle close and surrender. His chest filled with a constricting ache he dispatched with a cough.

"Jill's a sweet girl, you know." Luci picked at the weather stripping of the window. Once, saving the innocent had been as much a part of Luci's mission in life as it was his. But this situation and his presence here kicked Cole and his death square into the present and punted pain deep into her soft green eyes.

"That just makes it easier for him."

Luci nodded, a resignation. "Walk me through what he's done."

Dom didn't like to see defeat weigh her down like this. She'd already suffered so much. He wanted to make this as easy for her as possible, but wasn't sure how when she'd made it so clear there was no room for him in her life and never would be. He pushed the door on the passenger's side open. This time, she let him. "Sit a spell, Luce."

She hesitated, then climbed into the cab, folding her long legs as far away from him as she could. Her knees pressed close together. Her hands cupped the worndown white ovals on the knees of her jeans. Her gaze centered on her lap, as if even looking at him was unbearable. How often had he dreamed of those legs, of that hair, of her? She smelled of peppermint and something else, rosemary, maybe. He forced himself to lean away into the window rather than forward to sniff at the intriguing scent and the complex knot of emotion she tied in him.

"I need to get back to my son soon. Just give me the Cliff's Notes on this guy." She glanced at the clock on the dashboard. "You have half an hour."

Chapter Three

Dom reached back and pulled an envelope from behind his seat. He shuffled photographs, then handed her the top picture. The air in the cab had grown unbearably warm. Luci dragged her sweaty palms over the thighs of her jeans before she accepted the first bit of concrete proof that Jill was in danger.

"The first victim was Katheryn Chamber, twenty-six, from Seattle, Washington," Dom said, the rhythm of his voice soothing in spite of the harsh nature of his subject. "She was a dot-com millionaire, divorced with a seven-year-old son. Her blond husband went by the name of Wade Bilski and passed himself off as a U.S. Marshal. She met him on a day cruise to Canada and married him within a month. A month later, he left her with nothing, except her house and the stock that was in her son's name."

Dom plucked a second photograph from the pile and slid it across the seat. "The second victim was Sharlene Vardeman, twenty-nine, from San Diego, California. The bulk of her wealth came from the division of assets after her divorce from a Napa Valley winery heir. She also had a seven-year-old son. She met Wesley Ripp at a naval hospital charity function and married him within a few weeks. Her bald Navy SEAL left her before the end of the honeymoon. All she had left was her house, her son and whatever investments she'd had in her son's name."

A third photo arrived in her hands. She fumbled the pass with fingers that suddenly seemed too thick to move.

Dom cleared his throat. "Victim number three was Carissa Esslinger, twenty-seven, from Portland, Oregon. She inherited her wealth and managed to keep most of it after her divorce. She also had full custody of her seven-year-old son. Wayne Edgeman, her redheaded SWAT officer, pulled her out of her crushed car after a traffic accident while he was off-duty. Three weeks later, they were married. Five days later, he was gone and so were her savings and investments, except for those in her son's name."

Dom passed over a fourth picture. It weighed down her palm as if it were made of lead.

"Laynie McDaniels, twenty-nine, victim number four, had the misfortune to bump into Willis Morehouse at one of her parents' parties," Dom continued. "He was a visiting guest brought along by an invited guest. The border agent with his black hair and dark eyes swept her off her feet while they danced. The oil heiress gave him everything he wanted, except what was in her seven-year-old son's name. When he left her, hours after their return from their honeymoon, she chased him down and ended up dead."

Victim number five was Jill. And Luci already had a feeling where that story was heading. "Laynie McDaniels was the first woman to die after being scammed."

"We're floating around two theories about her death," Dom said, all business, as if they were back in a briefing room. That's what she'd wanted wasn't it? To keep this whole situation on a professional level?

"One," he continued, "is that she feared her parents' reaction to the squandering of her wealth and she ended her life rather than deal with the shame. Because the medical examiner's findings were inconclusive, the cops investigating the case felt the evidence pointed in that direction. The second theory is that she found her husband in the motel room where a maid discovered her hanging body and that he killed her."

"You told me she was killed, so you're siding with theory number two. Any evidence?"

Dom shook his head, his jaw tightening with frustration. "None that would impress a jury beyond a reasonable doubt. If Swanson was there that night, he did a good job cleaning up after himself."

"What about forensics at the scene?"

"An empty bottle of water in the wastebasket with Laynie's prints on it. At least a dozen unknown fingerprints. A common, everyday shirt button that could have belonged to any of the room's previous occupants."

"Who booked the room?" Luci asked, her mind trying to go back to a time when this kind of questioning was second nature.

"The registration was in another woman's name. Paid in cash."

"Could be anybody, then." Luci scanned Laynie's photograph. Laynie's dark brown eyes sparkled with joy and kindness—like Jill's. Luci bit the inside of her cheek pensively. She couldn't say why, but she was sure Laynie wouldn't have abandoned her son that way. Too cruel for such a soft woman. "Which brings me back to why did he kill her?"

"If we knew that, we'd be ahead of the game. Maybe she just couldn't let go and he felt he had to take that drastic measure to cut her off and move on."

Something didn't sound right. Luci flicked her braid over her shoulder. "What if she saw something she wasn't supposed to see? He took a different name with each woman. What if she'd discovered something about his next identity? What if that's the reason she ended up dead? If she could tell police who he was going to be next, then he couldn't afford to let her blab. What showed up between the time her husband disappeared and the time she was found?"

"She never woke up from her coma. We never got to talk to her personally. Everything in her file, we got secondhand from her mother and her friends. I'll let you read the interviews."

Aware of the heat discharging from Dom's body, she studied Laynie once again, wishing the dead woman could speak. "Did anyone look into her phone records?"

"Of course, we traced them back. Cell and landline. All her calls were to her mother. None after her teary call, saying that Willis had disappeared. We looked at her credit card purchases and came up with a gas receipt. Nothing else." Dom handed her four other photographs—men this time.

Luci lined up each "husband's" photo in a row. Warren had managed to keep the photographer far enough away that details were hard to extrapolate. "There's just enough difference to make you wonder if it's the same person or someone he happens to resemble."

Dom's hand brushed hers as he pointed out the differences. The heat of his skin jolted through her.

"The hairstyles and color change," Dom said. "So does the weight. These are things he can easily manipulate."

"But some things stay the same." Luci frowned and focused on the photos. She didn't have time to let herself get distracted by Dom and the shipwreck of emotions he seemed to raise from her. Jill's future depended on her figuring out the key that unlocked Warren's secrets.

"His eye color," Dom said. "He could use colored contacts, but for some reason, he doesn't. And each woman also described an Alpha Omega tattoo on his left pec."

"Hard to hide a tattoo from someone you're intimate with." Luci shuddered. Intimacy. Warren had gotten Jill into bed quickly and easily. "Is that part of his pattern? Using sex to dull any alarm bells that might try to ring?"

"It's worked five times so far."

Luci spread each photo of the various incarnations of Warren on the dashboard. Below, she placed a picture of his victims. "None of the women look similar. They range from tall to short, from plump to skinny, from blond to brunette."

"He's more interested in their investments than their looks."

"But still, there has to be some reason he picked them."

"Opportunity's a big part of it."

Luci twirled the end of her braid between her fingers. "But he seems to make his own opportunities—the cruise, the party. He bumped into Jill at the country club. He has to stalk them ahead of time to know where they're going to be, how to run into them in a way that doesn't spook them."

Dom raked both hands through his hair. "He likes water, so he heads for cities near the water. Bigger cities give him the cover to pop up in those places and make it look like fate."

"That doesn't fit Austin. Yes, it's a city, but it's not near water."

"Laynie's parents have a home on Galveston and a big yacht to cruise the gulf. That's where he met her."

The calm measure of his voice softened the jagged edges cutting hers, made her want to lean on him. She tried to ignore the buzz that heated her blood whenever his arm or his hand brushed close to her.

"Okay," Luci said, pressing the heels of her hands into her eyes, forcing herself to focus on Warren. "So he likes water. Why? What does it mean? That he was brought up near water? Jill said he was from Florida. Is that his home base?"

"Or his base of operations."

"What makes you think so?"

"The Social Security numbers." Dom listed them. "They all have the same first three numbers. What state do you think that prefix belongs to?"

"Florida?" she guessed.

He nodded once. "They're all real. They all belong to the name listed."

"I see dead people?"

Dom's rough bark of laughter rolled inside her like summer thunder. "No, they don't belong to dead people—just made-up ones."

"Okay, so he bought the Social Security numbers along with the rest of his ID in Florida or from someone with Florida connections. Florida's a big state with a lot of shoreline. How are we going to find his point of operation?"

Dom huffed out a breath that hinted at his frustration. "We'll keep combing the haystack until the sun hits the needle."

That would take time Jill didn't have. Somewhere in this information was a clue she was overlooking. Luci was sure of it. "Other than their large bank accounts, all the women had one other thing in common. A seven-year-old son."

Dom's mouth tightened. "The young child is part of his pattern. We're thinking that he sees the woman having a child as making her more vulnerable, an easier mark."

"Maybe, but I think there's more to it. Look at the pattern. Not just any young child. Always seven-year-old boys. Never a girl. Not six or eight or twelve. Always seven. There has to be a reason." Luci swallowed hard. The importance of that fact scraped her throat raw as it went down. "Jill has a seven-year-old boy."

Keeping his voice calm and cool, Dom told her how he'd followed the con man's footsteps from Texas, the place of his last con, along the coast to Louisiana, Alabama and Florida, waiting for a chance to catch him in the act. "He's armed, Luci. He hasn't used a weapon yet, but I've seen him carry."

She blew out a breath, just as if she were getting ready to squeeze a trigger. She'd tried to outrun herself, but beneath the harried suburbanite there still hid an expert marksman. He just had to remind her she'd once loved the hunt for justice.

"Do you know who he really is?" she asked, staring out the window as if she were scouting for the enemy.

"No. I'm still trying to work back to that."

She shifted her attention to his face. Her braid slinked forward over her shoulder like pale gold silk. The heat of her gaze burned all the way to his gut. He forced his shoulders to relax, his face to remain neutral, his pulse to slow.

An orange-streaked sky blazed behind her. The breeze ruffled the rough shear of the bangs that framed her eyes. His fingers itched to brush the strands back, to tangle with the wispy softness of her hair. He slipped his fingers beneath his thighs and waited.

"So what next?" she asked, gaze flicking back out the windshield of the truck.

The rules of negotiation were simple enough: know your opponent, understand the challenge, introduce new alternatives, set the rules and go for the agreement. He knew Luci, all right, knew what made her tick, what made her laugh, what made her cry. He understood that after Cole's death she'd tried to reinvent herself, that nothing could be the same. So he had to concentrate on her love for her family, on her worry for Jill, on her need to preserve her personal circle of safety. He had to make sure he gave her the opportunity to suggest alternatives. Working indirectly would work better with someone strong like Luci. And he somehow had to get her to agree to let him step back into her life, even though every minute in his presence would remind her of Cole and the way he'd died.

"Well, here's the stickler," Dom said, keeping his voice flat. "Even with a file full of this guy's predation, there isn't a D.A. in the country who'll want to take on the case unless I can prove he had criminal intent going in. Now you and I know that all he sees in Jill is dollar signs, but the D.A. feels the court will see only a fighting couple disagreeing on distribution of wealth. Not much sympathy for either party there from a jury. No D.A. will take on a case he doesn't feel he can win."

"If they can't get him on the scam, why don't they get him on identity fraud?"

Dom shrugged. "He doesn't steal his IDs. He builds them. Here, too, I need proof of criminal intent to defraud."

She flipped her braid back with a quick jerk of her hand. "So you're saying there's nothing we can do."

"There's plenty we can do, but we'll have to be imaginative about it. Now if I come in and confront this guy with accusations, no matter how many pieces of paper I can pull out of my file to prove my point, what do you think's going to happen?"

Luci waved about an invisible magic wand. "Presto, change-o, gone."

"Right. And I'd have to start all over again. So here's my quandary. How do I get close to a man who doesn't want to get close to anyone but his pigeon?"

Gaze narrowed, she still scoured the soccer fields and the edge of oaks and pines beyond as if she expected some sort of monster to pop up. "You play his game.

You get someone else, who isn't seen as a threat, to introduce you."

"Now you've got it."

A muscle rippled on Luci's tension-tight cheek. "And that's me."

"I need to get close to him, Luce. If I show up as your friend, he won't suspect I'm on his tail. He'll buy my presence and my attempt at friendliness. And if I stop him now, he won't hurt anyone else."

"How's that going to work? If he's as good as you say he is, won't he just look you up and know you're lying? After all, Jill says he's a private detective."

"Not the way I've got things set up."

"Are you using a pseudonym?" The skin on her knuckles was getting redder, the tips of her fingers whiter.

She may want to pretend she didn't care, but she did. And not just for Jill; for Swanson's possible next victim, too. "Easier to use my own name in this case because we have football in common. Gives us a starting position for conversation. Nothing shows I don't want to. What he'll find is that I'm an insurance salesman from Houston. He'll see I was just transferred to Holliday & Houghlin in Nashua."

"Won't he find a real estate deed for your current residence?"

"Nope, it's under a corporation name. On paper, Dominic Skyralov doesn't own a thing. Even this truck is a brand-new rental."

"So where am I supposed to say you're staying?" Her voice was pricklier than a bed of cacti.

"Well, darlin', that's where imagination comes in."

Eyes wide with panic, she jerked her head in his direction. Old hostilities bubbled up and spilled over. "No, absolutely not. I'm not inviting you to stay at my home. I have a young son to think about. That won't work."

Dom slung an arm carelessly over the back of the seat, trying to keep his body relaxed and nonthreatening. "Swanson's last mark is dead."

"Then stay with Jill. She's the one in danger. Not me."

"I don't think Swanson'd be too happy about that. He seems like the jealous type, especially now that he's so close to his prize."

"So how do I explain your presence in my home?"

Dom shrugged. "We're old friends, and you're letting me use your couch until I find a place to settle down. She's at the falling in love stage—everything is rosy and perfect. He's a good talker. Look at what he's already talked her into doing and he bumped into her only two weeks ago."

Watching Luci struggle with the conflict of hatred and love, of duty and fear, pulling her in two directions, cut hard. The last thing he'd wanted was to hurt her.

"Okay," she said, "come with me to dinner on Saturday."

Relief sagged the tense muscles of his stomach. "That's all I want, Luce. A chance to stop him before anyone else gets hurt."

She reached for the door and pushed it open. "Tell me what information you need. I'll get it for you while you talk to him."

"I'll need Jill's identifiers and the number of any account he could deplete. I'll have our computer expert put a flag on them. We'll be able to tell when he starts pilfering and catch him red-handed."

"Okay."

She started to scoot out and he held her back, the warm feel of her sweatshirt a treat for his fingers.

"Saturday dinner," she said, a cloud of pain dulling the green of her eyes. "That's all I can commit to right now."

"Well, darlin', at this point, I'll take anything I can get." Even if it wasn't nearly enough to satisfy him.

Her clogs crushed the gravel as she exited the truck. She looked him up and down. "Do you own anything other than jeans? My parents'll be there, too, and they don't approve of denim."

He let a grin bloom on one side of his face. "Tell you what, I'll even shower and shave. It'll be nice to see your folks again." The only time he'd met them was at Cole's funeral—not the best of circumstances. They'd probably forgotten the handshake and condolences. Cole had had so many friends, in and out of the Marshalls Service.

She shut the door, and letting her walk away, even after such a short time, hurt all over again.

After a few steps, she turned back, the ghosts of the past flitting in her eyes. "I was just getting over August, Dom. Why'd you have to come back?"

Dom stared at her eyes, reflecting his own demons back at him, then glanced away like a guilty man. Because August still weighed on his conscience, too. Cole's death was his fault and he couldn't bear the thought of her in pain again over someone she loved—

or that he couldn't be the man to comfort her. "To keep you safe and happy, Luce. That's all I've ever wanted."

DARK SURROUNDED HER, sucked at her, dragged her under. Her breath rasped in her ears. Sweat stuck T-shirt to skin, holding her prisoner in that airless black beneath the sheets. The more she fought, the tighter the bonds got, the thinner the air got. The smell of cordite and blood stung her nostrils, pinched her lungs. The ring of discharge scrambled her brain.

But even as she fought the dark, she pleaded for its protective cover. It never listened. The darkness always cleared, bringing soul-ripping pain that doubled her over with nausea.

Man down! Man down!

Cole. Right there in her scope. So close. So far away. His brown hair sticky with red. His brown eyes wide with surprise, lifeless. His blood a halo around his head. Dead.

Keeping him safe had been her job and she'd failed. When it had really mattered, all the training, all the practice, all the preparation had fallen short.

A fraction of a second. A millimeter of space.

And the man she'd loved was gone.

Her mistake. No matter how she looked at it. Her fault.

She'd proved in the most graphic of ways she wasn't good enough.

She'd thought of giving up, of letting the darkness take her along with Cole, but Cole, with his life-lived-to-the-utmost wish, would have disapproved. Then there was Brendan, the tiny seed there in her belly.

Cole hadn't known. She barely had.

For a while, she'd only gone through the motions, been nothing but a living dead. Dom's voice, always Dom's voice, calm and cool, trying to talk her back into the horrid world she'd created.

Her husband was dead. His child grew in her womb. So she did the only thing she could; she ran.

She ran from city to city, looking for something, anything that would connect her to a sense of support. But every time she'd thought she'd found salvation, it crumbled beneath her feet, leaving her weaker than before. She couldn't outrun the ghosts. They chased her everywhere—her mother's reproach, her husband's bloody body, her friend's hypnotic voice.

Then Brendan was born and she'd had to find a higher level of functioning for his sake. Moving from place to place had made no sense. So she'd come home. The farm and its constant need for toil had saved her.

Living still hurt. But she was holding her little world together and Brendan was growing up into a happy boy with a zest for life as big as his father's. She would do everything in her power to keep him safe.

A glance at the clock's red numbers showed her she'd gotten a few hours' worth of sleep. She tossed off the sweat-dampened sheet and blanket. Four in the morning wasn't that early. From experience she knew sleep was done for the night. Lying in bed would mean sleeping with ghosts.

Bleary-eyed, she made her way to the bathroom with its sea-colored tiles and crawled under the showerhead, letting warm water wash away the sticky filaments of her nightmare.

She had enough goat's milk left over to cook up a batch of soap. Might as well get started. She had the pesto, herb logs and vinaigrette she'd made last night to deliver later this morning. Maybe she'd make an outing out of it and take Brendan out for pancakes at The Sugar Barn. Then she had the breeding for Fanny, Faye and Fiona, her dairy goats, to arrange, the green manure to sow in her gardens and the greenhouses to finish setting up. Not to mention the torte she'd promised to bake for Jill's shindig this afternoon. If she were lucky, she'd be tired enough to sleep again tonight.

Luci buffed her body dry with a towel, left the bathroom and slipped on a sweatshirt and work jeans. Her head pounded in a drum that beat in time to the queasy roll in her stomach. Work would take care of that; it always did.

Before going downstairs, she peeked in on Brendan. Maggie, sleeping at the foot of the bed, lifted her head and banged her tail against the footboard in a way that said, "Guilty as charged. Can I stay?"

Brendan was lying sheets akimbo as if he'd fought off an army of dream monsters. Cole had been like that, too, active even in sleep. With his eyes closed, her son looked like his father—spikes of dark hair, a ready-to-smile mouth, a stubborn square chin that told the world he knew what he wanted and no one was going to get in his way. The only thing Brendan had inherited from her was his green eyes. His looks made forgetting Cole impossible. But none of her guilt would taint her son if she could help it.

Without turning on a light, she made her way down the stairs to the kitchen, where she slipped on her barn clogs and grabbed a flashlight from the windowsill. Outside, September chill wriggled its fingers into the weave of her sweatshirt, raising goose bumps. Soon, the first killing frost would come. She had a lot of work to do before then.

As she stepped into the yard, more than the coolness of the night shivered down her spine. Something or someone had disturbed the equilibrium of her farm's peaceful atmosphere. She flashed her light around the yard, but could see nothing out of place.

Reverting to old technique, she turned off the light and edged her way to the barn in a toes-to-heel stride that kept her footfalls near silent. The well-oiled barn door slid smoothly on its runners. She knew the location of every shadow, every scent, every movement. Finding the one out of place didn't take long. She moved in on it, slowly but surely.

Dom.

He slept on a bed of straw in the empty stall near the enclosure the goats shared. Fanny and Faye ignored him, but doeling Fiona seemed intrigued by the hair she couldn't quite reach through the wooden planks with her tongue. Wrinkles pleated his forehead, as if his sleep wasn't any more restful than hers. Was Cole haunting him, too?

Was the menacing growl of Dom's truck what had started her dream? Why was he here? Hadn't he caused enough trouble for one day?

The sight of Dom there, his big body lax in sleep knocked her back as if someone had pulled a carpet from beneath her feet. Memories seeped through the wall of pain her mind fought to keep up. Dom's soothing voice. Cole's bright laugher. The friendly kidding, the easy camaraderie that turned into fierce support when needed. How often had she woken up to find Dom sacked out on the couch, looking just like this?

No one had wanted her on the team, least of all Cole. But Dom had played negotiator from the start and, somehow, the three of them had become the best of friends. Those four years on the team were the best in her life and part of her yearned for that easy companionship.

For that brief reprieve in time, she'd belonged.

She clutched the flashlight more tightly in her hand. *Don't go there, Luci. That's not the answer.*

She flicked the switch on the flashlight and shone its light in Dom's face. "What are you doing here?"

Dom jolted upright, ready to defend himself, then relaxed when he realized whose voice had roused him from a deep sleep. "I should've known you'd find me."

He lifted a hand to shield his eyes from the bright light. "What are you doing up so early?"

Why don't you sit a spell, Luce, tell me what's on your mind? How often had Dom said that to her with his molasses drawl? How often had she done exactly that? Sagged into the comfort of his broad chest and cried her eyes out, spilling out her sad secrets while he listened without reproach? *I'm trying to outrun nightmares. You should know that by now.* But he was the last person she needed to share these dark dreams with. "This is a working farm. I work."

"Not usually this early." He rose, brushing straw from his jeans.

She flashed the light back into his eyes. "You've been watching me?"

"I had to weigh, Luce," he said, taking the flashlight from her hand and resting it on top of the stall wall. "I had to figure out which would hurt you less, breaking my promise to you or working around you to try to help your sister."

That was one thing about Dom, he was a man of his word. After he'd coached her through Brendan's birth, and while she was still swimming in post-partum hormones, she'd made him promise never to see her again. He'd kept his word these past six years. Even with felons, he went with truth as often as he could. Using people wasn't his style. He wanted everyone comfortable and happy.

That wasn't apt to happen this time. Jill was going to get hurt, and nothing would ever quite be the same. "That still doesn't explain why you're entertaining my goats with your snores."

He wiped one hand over his mouth as if reluctant to admit the truth. "Guilt. I let you down. I need to know you'll be okay."

Guilt she could understand. She sagged on a bale of straw outside the stall, the wooden wall still between them, and clasped her hands around one knee. "I talked to Renwick last night."

Picking up the phone had taken much more courage than Luci cared to admit. After her less-than-cozy chat with her old boss, she'd stayed up past midnight, too hyped up on adrenaline and worry to find her way around to sleep.

"That couldn't have been easy. Especially after the

way he treated you." Renwick had not been amused by Luci's and Cole's secret wedding. Rules strictly forbid family from working on the same team.

A note of hurt cracked the low, slow richness of Dom's voice. "You thought I'd lied?"

"I—" Her shoulder lifted in a hesitant jerk. Sharing Brendan's birth with him had bonded them in a way that had scared her. Turning to him then had been a moment of weakness she couldn't repeat. The last thing she'd needed was a reminder of her failure every day of her life. The sight of Dom would always pull along the memory of Cole. She wasn't strong enough to endure that torture. "I had to hear it from someone else."

"Fair enough."

She picked at the hole starting to fray on the knee of her jeans. "How'd Warren—or whoever he is—find Jill?"

"Her divorce probably made the papers. The Walden and the Courville names often make the society pages. She makes an easy target." Dom leaned his forearms against the top of the stall and looked down at her. "I'll do this however you want, Luci. I won't let you or your sister get hurt."

She could kid herself that the past didn't matter. But it did. Every day she lived with that truth. She had to wash Cole's blood out of her eyes every morning before she could put on her mom-skin for Brendan. And every time she looked at her son's dark hair and smiling face, guilt pinged in her heart. She'd taken his father from him. He'd missed out on what fathers and sons did together, those manly rituals a woman could never hope to understand. J.J., Jill's ex, was a good father to

Jeff, but he'd never wanted to include Brendan in their father-and-son times.

Every instinct sharpened and honed by grief shouted that allowing Dom to stay was a mistake. Another vivid reminder that her son was growing up without a father. But her arrogance had already cost her the man she loved. She couldn't risk her sister's life because of pride. For Jill, she'd endure the torture. "The guest room is off the living room. I'll get you some clean sheets."

Chapter Four

In the darkest hour before dawn, Dom followed Luci to the back door of the old Victorian house. A single light out on the front porch made a soft halo appear to shimmer around it.

She walked across the packed dirt with an economy and efficiency of movement he'd often admired. He matched her stride with the ease of familiarity even six years of absence couldn't erase, wishing she'd lean on him as she once had. Her tall and lanky body paired his at the hip, shoulder and head. He'd always liked that she was equal to him like that, eye to eye, heart to heart. Her ramrod posture betrayed her inbred country club etiquette and the military-like training Special Operations Groups endured.

She pushed open the back door, and the squeak of spring on the outer screen reminded him of home. He needed to call his parents and touch base. The anniversary of Nate's death was creeping around the corner. Losing their eldest son so tragically had aged both his parents prematurely. They seemed to grow more brittle with each passing year.

Luci turned and held the door for him, the scent of

her herbal soap a balm to his tired senses. Her narrow face was set and unreadable, except for the wariness and emotional exhaustion in her eyes. He couldn't blame her. He must seem like the omen from hell, appearing out of the blue like that and bringing out all the demons she'd tried so hard to beat back.

"I can sleep in the barn," he said, hand on the cold doorknob. If he could redo that day seven years ago— but no, he had to live with his mistakes. The least he could do was to make his presence here as painless as possible for Luci.

"What would the neighbors say?" She crooked one half of her mouth, bitterness rolling off her tongue so softly it took a moment before its acid burned.

She stepped out of her green rubber clogs and brushed by him before heading out toward the deeper recesses of her home.

"Forget the sheets," he said, letting the unexpected longing the accidental graze sparked in him settle. "It's too late for sleep."

She hesitated, turned around and, at the white Formica counter, flipped the switch on the coffeemaker. It gurgled and hissed, then dripped, counting the seconds stretching between them. He hadn't wanted to disturb her hard-gained peace, but if he was right, then the rage that drove Swanson's obsession to ruin divorced women was escalating and what happened to Laynie McDaniels could happen to Jill. Dom would do everything he could to save Luci from losing her sister the way he'd lost his brother—the way they'd both lost Cole.

Under her skin, pale with fatigue, was a classic bone structure. Even etched with the weight of years of grieving, her features evoked an unyielding strength of character. Luci was a survivor, but even survivors needed support now and then.

He swallowed the ache of emotion he'd fought at Cole's funeral, at Brendan's birth and most days since Luci had made him promise to steer clear. He'd fought the pull Luci had on him and stayed away—more as an act of penance than an ethical duty.

"Do you want to talk now or later?" he asked, leaning against the door and mirroring her crossed arms and crossed ankles. There was no way to soften all the little darts he'd have to throw her way in the next few days.

She plucked two mugs from a doorless cupboard. She placed them on the counter and held on to them, as if to anchor herself, while the coffee continued to drip into the pot. "Like I said, this is a working farm. In a bit, I'll have goats to milk and feed."

"I can help."

"That's not necessary."

"I want to."

"I don't."

She'd talked herself through pain before. But Luci had refused to talk about Cole and his death. Still did.

Doing what they'd done, they'd known the risks going in and accepted them. Luci's living death, that was something else.

He wanted to take her in his arms, as he'd done so often while she was grieving Cole, lay her head against his heart and let the vibrations of her voice seep into his blood and into his bones.

If he'd—*No, stick to Jill. Forget the rest.*

"Talk to me about Jill," Dom said as Luci poured the fragrant brew into the mugs.

"Don't you have everything you need in your files?"

She handed him a mug and, like a glutton for punishment, he reached for the coffee he didn't want, deliberately skimming his fingers against hers, letting the brief contact sigh inside him.

"I have the black and white. I need the gray."

"You always did have a way with words." She leaned her trim rear against the counter once more, closed her eyes, shutting him out as if even looking at him was too painful to bear, and sipped. "Ask your questions. I'll try to answer."

"Does Jill have life insurance?"

"I would imagine she does, but I don't know."

"What's the source of her income?"

Luci swallowed hard, scrunching her closed eyes even tighter. "Aside from child support, mostly investments. If Warren wiped her out, she'd end up in a bad fix."

The tautness of her jaw made him think she was imagining the possible destruction of Jill's life. Jill wasn't as strong as her sister; that's why she'd made an easy mark. Swanson would never pick someone like Luci—too much work. "What do you know about her investments?"

"Not much." Regret tainted her voice as she blinked her eyes open. "Jill and I have always had a prickly relationship. The boys are what allowed us to get closer these past few years."

Luci had shed a gallon of tears on his shoulder over the way her family had stayed away after Cole's death. He didn't want to take those freshly renewed ties away from her. "What about her mortgage or any other loans?"

"J.J., that's Jill's ex-husband, paid off the house as part of their divorce settlement. She owns it free and clear. All she has to worry about is the taxes and the interest from her investments pays that. As far as I know, she doesn't have any other outstanding loans."

"Does her investment interest cover the rest of her bills, too?"

Luci nodded. "She also gets a generous monthly child support check."

"Does she get along with her ex?"

"As well as can be expected when your husband leaves you for an older woman." Luci gave up on the coffee and bricked up her protective shield by crossing her arms. "What exactly are you after here?"

"I'm looking for patterns."

"See any?" A hint of fear warbled through her voice.

"For him, yeah. Jill's situation follows the perfect template, right down to the young child. And it looks like most of her assets are the kind he'd be able to talk her into signing him on as beneficiary or co-owner."

Her gaze snapped to the ceiling as if she were seeing right through the layers of Sheetrock and flooring and into her son's room. She'd do anything to protect her son—and Jill's, too. The innocents, they'd always been her number one concern. "He wouldn't hurt Jeff, would he?"

"So far, he's always left the kids alone. He doesn't touch what's theirs." But Swanson took abnormal glee in watching his pigeons flounder and flail, in watching them fall. "This is the closest I've managed to get to him."

"What are you hoping to get this afternoon?"

Dom shrugged. "His passion, his personality, his Achilles' heel. Something that'll trip him up. If I can get him to talk about something that's real, maybe I can trace him back, find out where he's from and where he's going. What it is he really wants."

Luci straightened, her eyes rounding with horror. "Oh, no."

"What?"

The beat of her fear pulsed at her neck. "Two weeks from tomorrow."

"What about it?"

Her hands reached back for the counter and hung on to it as if she were suddenly dizzy. "Jill turns twenty-nine."

"And?"

The knuckles of both hands whitened. "The trust fund my grandfather set up for her reverts to her then."

"How much?"

"Over a million by now. And she can do with it anything she pleases."

The unspoken—*even hand it over to a con man*—hung in the air like frost.

"That's Jeff's future," Luci said.

Just as Dom suspected, Luci had used her trust fund to secure Brendan's.

Another innocent victim. Even if Jill were walking into Swanson's con willingly, Jeff wasn't. With that, Dom had secured Luci's partnership. For both of them, the exercise would be hell. "We won't let him take it away."

ALL THIS STRESS, Luci decided as she discarded yet another outfit after lunch, wasn't good for her. A barbed wire fence wasn't as tightly wound as she was at the moment. The last thing she wanted to do was snap—especially in front of her mother. And this, she thought, looking into the oval mirror above her dresser, wasn't helping. With each new dress or skirt, she could imagine her mother's objections. "That yellow isn't the most flattering color on you, Lucinda. That dress is ten years out of style. Perhaps if you did something with your hair."

Too gawky to have grown into the elegant and graceful society swan her mother had desired, Luci had stood a head above her classmates until college, when a few of the boys had caught up with her. In dresses and high heels, she was an awkward duck, but in shorts and sneakers, she could stand up to anyone on the volleyball court, basketball court and softball diamond. Which led her to the U.S. Marshals Service and the Hostage Rescue Team, something her mother had never accepted, but that her father had secretly cheered.

Luci tugged on the pumpkin-orange silk dress and set the hanger clanging against its neighbors.

Holding the dress draped across her front, Luci braved another look into the mirror. This wasn't going to work, either. Too formal for a family barbecue. She dropped the dress on the wide pine floorboards, looked into her closet and sighed. She'd run out of options all the way around. She snatched the last item left hanging in her closet—a red moleskin skirt. From the dresser, she pulled an old apple-green cardigan. That would have to do.

As she raked fingers through her hair to unwind her braid, laughter streamed up the stairs—Brendan's boisterous one and Dom's deeper one.

Don't think about Dom downstairs with Brendan. Think about Jill and Jeff and that scum pond Warren.

If she were a dirtbag going around pretending she

was someone she wasn't and building up another identity for the next scam, where would she do her dastardly deed? Sitting on the edge of her bed, she ran a brush through her hair, then replaited the strands. No place where anyone could catch the double life, so probably not at his showplace office or whatever rat's nest he called home. So where did Warren The Worm hide his sticky dealings? She'd let that percolate in her subconscious. Maybe by the time she got home, she'd have an answer.

She found Dom and Brendan in the living room, zapping alphabet aliens on the computer. Maggie kept butting her head against Dom's hand and her flapping tail swirled hair onto his black pants. Great, now her mother would also have Dom to criticize. Maybe for once her mother's gaze wouldn't go farther than Dom's hypnotizing blue-jeans eyes and she'd forget to look for imperfection. As she had with Cole the few times they'd met.

"We'll take my van," Luci said, wanting some sort of control over the situation. The truck cab was too narrow with its one long seat. She needed space between them. "Brendan, go find your shoes."

"Aw, Mo-om. Can't we take the truck? Dom said we could."

"No." She aimed her son toward the stairs. "And see if you can connect a brush with your hair."

Dom stirred a hand through Brendan's dark hair as he went by. "Next time, sport."

Brendan whined and clomped his way up the stairs.

Next time? No, no next time if she could help it. She'd get the information Dom needed and end this torture as soon as possible. There was no need to prolong this agony of forced proximity. Not with Cole, the two-ton albatross they couldn't discuss, sitting between them.

When the van's bucket seats proved to be too close also, she fought the urge to bolt from the vehicle and return to the relative haven of the barn. The calming rhythm of chores, that's what she needed, not Dom's sinful drawl next to her as he entertained Brendan with wild stories of chasing after bad guys with his sheriff father.

"Luce, you okay?" Dom asked as she popped the parking brake and shoved the van in gear. The friendly brush of his fingers against her shoulders to catch her attention only ratcheted her nerves up another notch.

"I'm just peachy." He could read right through her tight smile, but she didn't care, and he was wise enough not to pursue the matter. This afternoon was going to be about as entertaining as eating nails. "Hold on to the torte. I'm told it's Warren's favorite."

"Then I'll take extra special care of it." He lifted the foil-wrapped torte to his nose. "Smells great."

Jill's house was everything that Luci's wasn't. Only two years old, it contained every convenience that one could imagine. Forest-green and cranberry trim accented the cashew shake-shingle siding. The house sat on Thoreau Lane, on a half-acre piece of land that worked hard to look natural but took a small army of landscapers to trim into shape. The lot over-looked the twelfth hole of Marston Country Club golf course. Her backyard faced the Nashua River and the wall of windows at the back of the house made the view seem like a moving painting. Today the scene was a portrait in gray—gray slate veranda, gray water, gray sky.

The scent of autumn-spice potpourri greeted them with a warm welcome. Jill's smile emitted enough electricity to light up the gloom of the day. She wore riding boots, a black riding skirt and a red suede vest that made her look as if she'd just come back from a hunt, even though those boots had never stepped on horse apples or that skirt sat a saddle. Her blond-highlighted bob made a sleek and perfect frame around her gamine face. "You must be the mystery man in the burgundy truck. I'm Jillian Courville. Call me Jill."

"Not so much mystery, Jill. Dominic Skyralov." A great big smile decorating his good-old-boy face, he gave a little bow and presented her the torte as if it were a royal treasure. "Call me Dom."

Jill, as most women did, batted her eyelashes at him. "Where has Luci kept you hidden?"

"I'm fresh up from Houston."

"Well, I hope you'll stick around for a while. Luci needs some shaking up, and you seem like just the person who could do it."

The problem was that if Dom did too much shaking, Luci would break apart. And that wouldn't do anyone any good.

Brendan dashed ahead to Jeff's room where they would no doubt play video games on Jeff's state-of-the-art system and stay out of the way of the stuffy adults.

"I like him," Jill whispered as she dragged Luci into the gleaming peach and stainless steel kitchen. A man stood at the granite counter pressing hamburger meat into patties. The salmon was already marinating in a glass dish.

Before Jill could make introductions, the doorbell rang again—a perfect three-toned chime. She slid the torte onto the counter and said, "I'll be right back. Warren, introduce yourself."

Warren washed his hands and came toward them, as if he had nothing to hide. Luci had expected a used-car salesman slickness about him, but he was just an average guy. His fine espresso-colored hair was cut in a neat style. His dove-gray fitted silk dress shirt, complete with mother-of-pearl cufflinks, went well with his designer-label charcoal pants and his black leather loafers, yet the cut of his cheekbones and the jut of his chin still gave him that noir edge Jill would find intriguing. His milk-chocolate eyes made contact with Luci's, reflecting warmth and confidence. Country-club clean, movie-star good-looking and boy-next-door charming. Luci had to give him points for knowing his target inside out.

"Hi! You must be Luci." He extended a hand, leaning toward her. Warmth spilled from him like a waterfall and flowed into her, jarring her with a feeling of instant connection she hadn't expected. "It's so nice to finally meet you, Luci. I'm Warren."

"It's nice to meet you, too." *I'd love to know your real name and why you want to hurt Jill.* She turned to Dom, who stepped forward, extending a hand. "This is my friend, Dominic Skyralov."

"Nice to meet you, Dominic. Can I offer you something to drink? Beer, wine, soda?"

"Thanks, Warren," Dom said, ratcheting up the drawl

in his voice. Why was he playing up the redneck? So Warren would feel superior? "A beer'll hit the spot."

All this fake rapport building was why Luci had gone to sniper school instead of negotiator school. As a sniper, silence was golden and that suited her just fine. She'd leave the talking to Dom. She was better at the stealth part, anyway—at least once upon a time.

Jill returned to the kitchen with Barbara and Neil Walden in tow. Their parents were dressed for this Saturday afternoon family barbecue as if they were attending some business lunch at the club. Her mother wore a tweed suit in shades of autumn and her father his usual black suit and red-striped power tie. Introductions were made all around. Dom managed to charm a smile out of her mother in spite of the dog hair decorating his pants. But Warren trumped him by offering to take her mother's jacket and purse and dropped both on the chair by the telephone table in the hallway.

Barbara gave Luci a quick hug, more air than body, enveloping her in a cloud of Guerlain, then held on to her wrists while she inspected her eldest daughter. "Lucinda, you're here already."

Luci bit her tongue and reminded herself her mother meant well and that, yes, lately, she'd run even later than usual at everything. "I have to leave by seven to get home in time to milk the goats."

Her mother tilted her head, not moving a single hair on her shellacked chestnut curls, and her hazel eyes filled with that special sadness she saved just for Luci. "Why don't you hire a farmhand to do those nasty chores?"

"Because I like doing those chores." Those nasty chores helped save her soul every day.

"I've offered to pay for part-time help," Barbara said, tucking a stray strand of hair behind Luci's ear.

She means well behind all that smothering, Luci reminded herself yet again. "I'm fine, Mom."

"You look tired. Maybe if you had a little help...you could enjoy your time with Brendan a little more."

Ouch. "Thanks, Mom, I appreciate your concern, but Brendan and I spend plenty of time together." Working hard through August was better than sinking too deeply into herself. But her mother couldn't see that, not when she'd never cared for Cole.

"Just think about it."

Jill rolled her eyes behind her mother's back. Then, becoming the dutiful daughter, she handed both parents their usual drinks—a gin and tonic for her father and glass of red wine for her mother. "Why don't we all go into the living room? There's still a bit of time before Warren starts the grill." Jill hooked an arm through her father's. "Daddy, you'll have to tell Warren all about your pilot days. He used to fly, too. Little planes, not jets like you."

"So what did you fly?" her father asked Warren.

"Pipers mostly," Warren said and swiftly took Jill's hand in his. Staking his claim? "It's been a while, though."

In the living room, with its dark beams, cream-colored walls and massive fieldstone fireplace, Jill plastered herself against Warren on the butter-yellow leather love seat, hand still twined with his, resting her head on his shoulder and glowing as if she had a fever. Her parents took the sofa, sitting as if they were preparing for some sort of battle.

Barbara dragged a hand down part of Luci's braid as Luci went by. "Lucinda, why don't you take my appointment with the hairdresser's on Monday? Susan's very good."

"Thanks, Mom, but you might as well keep it." Luci flicked her braid over her shoulder with the back of a hand and she sat in the snot-green armchair Jill called celadon. "This is easy to take care of."

"It's an open offer. Let me know."

"It'd be a shame to cut such glorious hair." Dom cupped a hand around the base of her neck, managing to both bubble heat through her pulse and calm the crater of anger her mother could stir up without even trying. How long since she'd had that kind of support? Too long. But that realization only served to sit her closer to the edge of panic. She couldn't start depending on Dom. She couldn't seek comfort in his touch.

The whole situation was wrong. Tension shouldn't wind through family parties, putting everyone on edge. Everyone should feel free to be themselves. Laughter should ring. Joy should waft in the air. It shouldn't be this sitting on thin ice, waiting for something or someone to crack. And she just might be the one if Dom kept stroking the back of her neck. She had to go and regroup herself before facing the next round of social pleasantries.

Luci grabbed her purse and excused herself. Now was as good a time to make an exit as any. "I'm going to go check on the boys. They need to get a bit of fresh air before the rain starts."

Barbara swallowed a sip of wine and placed the glass on a coaster. "They'll get dirty."

That's what little boys do, Mom. "They won't sit still at the table if they don't run off some energy."

Without waiting for a reply, Luci strode into the hallway, tears prickling her eyes. Why was she letting her mother get to her? She should have gotten over the need to please her mother after all these years of trying without success. She slipped into the library, across the hall from the stairs leading upstairs and closed the door behind her. She didn't spare the well-stocked shelves a look. Most of the leather-bound books were for show, not substance.

Luci headed for the desk J.J., Jill's rotten ex, had chosen for mass rather than function. To give J.J. his due, he'd kept meticulous records. Luci reached for the bottom left-hand drawer where the financial files were stored. But the drawer didn't move. Crouching, she found the reason—a shiny new lock. Sniffing, she pawed through the rest of the drawers, but located no key. Why did Jill have that drawer locked? That wasn't like her. Shaking her head to clear the tears, Luci chose a thin blade from the pocketknife in her purse, then tried to finesse the lock.

A moment later, the lock gave way with a satisfying click. But her victory was short-lived. An alarm shrilled from the drawer. Closing the thing only served to muffle the noise, not kill it. Pulse skittering madly, she pressed at buttons on the keypad poking up from the black metal plate covering the drawer's inside.

Jill came running in, followed by Dom. "What happened?"

"I was looking for a tissue." Bent over the drawer, Luci swatting at the tears of frustration that had spilled over. Tiredness, that's all. It made her oversensitive. "You used to keep a big box in there and—"

Jill punched in a few numbers on the keypad and the noise stopped. "I had a safe installed there."

"A safe?" Luci sniffed, silently telegraphing to Dom her failure to obtain the information he needed. His gaze conveyed more worry than disappointment.

"Warren suggested that some of my jewelry was too valuable to stay exposed in my jewelry box," Jill said, showing off her latest acquisition.

So now Warren knew which pieces were worth taking and which weren't and exactly where to find them. Probably knew the secret numbers to pop that baby open, too.

"Tissues are here." Jill swiveled to the credenza behind the desk and bent down to retrieve a box of tissues from one of the cupboards.

"You okay?" Dom whispered, sending a shiver snaking down Luci's spine. He cupped her elbow with one hand, the soothing heat of his touch bleeding into her. With the other, he dabbed at her tears with a handkerchief. Her heart ached at the tenderness of his touch, at her unexpected yearning to lean into it. Fresh tears gathered and swam. She couldn't do this. Dom might have forgiven her for what had happened to Cole, but she never could.

"I'm fine," she said, but to her horror, her voice warbled.

Jill turned, tissue box in hand. "Oh, looks like you've got it under control." She patted Luci's arm with the tips of her red fingernails. "Don't let Mom get to you."

Luci nodded. Guilt tugged at her conscience. She didn't like lying to her sister. Since the boys' births, half a year apart, they'd finally started to have a decent relationship. These lies would ruin it. But she wasn't going to let some jerk without a moral compass take away Jill's security. One Walden with a black view of the world was enough.

Luci tried to maneuver out of Dom's too-close-for-comfort hold, but he slid his hand around her waist, tripping a whole battalion of alarms as he went. Once his hand reached her hip, he pulled her closer so that they stood side by side with what, to Jill, must look like more than friendship. Luci couldn't waltz out of his embrace without making a scene and having Jill wonder at her reaction, so she forced out a rough laugh and tried to get the show back on track. "J.J. would have a fit if he knew you'd gotten rid of his master filing system."

"I made my own." A foxlike satisfaction crooked a smile on Jill's face. She opened the credenza's other cupboard door and showed off her multicolored file folders with their neat titles. "Blue for Jeff, red for me, green for accounts and yellow for maintenance."

"I'm impressed." The scent of Dom's cologne, like a fresh breeze, seemed to wrap around her and derail her thoughts right off their track.

"I took a course on finance for the single woman," Jill continued, oblivious to Luci's plight.

Too bad they hadn't gone over how to protect herself from two-legged, charming frauds. Trying to gather her thoughts, Luci honked into Dom's handkerchief. That proved too close to a caress when the same cool, clean scent that lingered on his skin imbued the linen.

"Are you going to be all right?" Jill asked, her gaze ping-ponging from Dom to Luci.

"Yeah, just give me a minute."

"I'll make sure she's okay," Dom said and leaned his head against hers. Luci realized then that Dom was putting on a show meant to get Jill to leave them alone.

"Okay, I'll cover for you." Jill nodded, eyes full of I've-got-a-secret pleasure. "I'll leave you in Dom's capable hands."

Jill's sweetness only served to tighten the painful hand of guilt around Luci's throat, the knot of unfaithfulness in her stomach.

Luci spun out of Dom's embrace and shook off her too-sharp awareness him. It butted against too many of her defenses. Defenses she needed to keep up to make it through the rest of her life without Cole. She crouched near the files and reached for the small notebook she kept in her purse. "You'd better get out there, so nobody wonders what's going on in here."

"What are you afraid of, Luci?"

She had to shut off her feelings, view her family, Dom, her betrayal of Jill's privacy as if they were part of an operation. Her goal, as it had always been as part of the team, was to provide an extra layer of protection for the assault team. Be ready to kill, but avoid shooting at all cost.

Discipline. Control. Restraint.

This time, she couldn't fail.

She met Dom's gaze of endless blue, pinned on a smile and told the biggest lie of all. "I'm not afraid of anything."

Chapter Five

"Your little lady sent me out with these salmon steaks." Dom handed the glass dish to Warren who was scraping bits of hamburger meat from the grill. The grill was a killer with built-in granite sideboards and two sets of oak cabinets beneath. "When'll you be ready for them?"

Swanson pulled a rack with holes from a cupboard under the grill, examined it, then placed it on the hot grill. "Give me a minute to warm up the rack."

Dom glanced over his shoulder at the wall of windows behind him, hoping to catch a glimpse of Luci. He hadn't liked the hard edge to her features when he'd left her in the library. Luci had never been that steely, not even in the field, or that fragile—until Cole's death. With reluctance, he tipped one of the two bottles of beer he carried, offering one to Swanson. This con man was the reason for this whole exercise. The sooner he brought Swanson down, the sooner he could end Luci's misery. "You look comfortable at the grill."

Swanson uncapped the bottle and pocketed the cap. "Old family tradition."

"Learned it from your father?" Dom parked himself across from Swanson and studied the overall pattern of the man's body movements. He straightened from his tendency to slouch to match Swanson's upright posture. Slowly, subtly, Dom started to mirror, raising his beer to his lips when Swanson did.

Swanson took a long draft to hide the tension sliding his jaw back and forth. "You could say that."

A tender spot. What had happened to the boy to make him grit his teeth at the mention of his father? Dom let his gaze turn back to the house, thought he caught sight of Luci's braid flashing through the dining room. Tender spots were weaknesses an adversary could use. Something he needed to remember. He'd gotten Luci's help not to put her in danger's way, but to get her sister and nephew out of it. "Nice family, the Waldens."

"How long have you known Luci?"

Dom let Swanson think he was in control of the conversation. For now. "We went to school together for a spell. Haven't seen her in years." She'd sent him packing the day Brendan had been born and had made him promise he'd never try to see her again. The punch of the pang in his gut came as a surprise, considering how he'd failed both her and Cole. "Didn't know what I was missing. Of course, she was married for a while."

"I understand her husband was killed on duty."

"Tough way to lose a loved one."

Swanson sprayed the pan on the grill with nonstick spray. "Jill has a generosity of spirit that sparkles, considering how her husband left her. I admire her resiliency."

"Looks like these women get their strength from their family ties. There's a lot of love between all these people. Makes a man want to settle down." Using a taste of his beer as cover, Dom pivoted his body to eyeball his target. *I'm not going to let your evil tear apart this family.* "Have you tried it before?"

"What?" Swanson speared a salmon steak with a long-handled fork and placed it on the grill where it sizzled and smoked.

"Marriage."

Swanson's eyes shifted to construct mode, down and right—a lie was coming. About what Dom had expected, along with the jerkiness of movement as Swanson plunked another steak on the grill.

"Never found the right person. Takes someone special. You? You tried it?"

"Yeah, once." Dom had tried to go through the motions after Luci pushed him away. Tammy had wanted marriage, and he'd liked her well enough to give it a shot. But a year into it, he'd realized that he craved the physical closeness, and every time he closed his eyes, it was Luci he took into his arms. Tammy deserved better than that. Fortunately, she'd agreed and they'd parted ways amicably. "I really miss having someone waiting at home."

"What happened?"

"The mostly nights and weekends of work didn't go over too well when she worked days. And when I couldn't give her kids." He shrugged. An outright lie, but he wanted to get Swanson's take on Jill's son.

"Yeah, I know how that goes."

Interesting that he'd skipped right over the kid. "That Jeff, he's a pistol."

Swanson switched to a spatula and concentrated on

getting the salmon steaks just right on the grill. His eyes flinched as if someone had pinched him. The recovery was quick, but a touch of sadness lingered. Was Luci right? Was the kid the smoking gun? If, so, then how? And how could he possibly trace back this man's childhood when he couldn't make a proper identification?

"I understand you're a private investigator," Dom tried again. "Regular hours probably don't work too well there, either."

"Most of my cases are locates for insurance companies and lawyers. It's mostly computer work, so I set my own hours."

"That's what I'm aiming for, too. Setting my own hours." They both sipped their beers. "Hey, I've just hired on with Holliday & Houghlin. Are they one of your clients?"

"Not yet."

"Well, if you're looking for more work, I'll pass your name on. Do you have a card?"

Swanson placed the spatula on the small granite counter on the side of the grill, pulled a wallet out of his back pocket and handed him a card. Rich vanilla with raised embossing in brown. Quality, heavy feel to it. Snappy, old-time design. Gate City Investigative Services, Inc. Generic enough. Swanson couldn't help wanting to get noticed, but didn't want to make too much of a splash.

"How long have you been doing this kind of work?" Dom asked, slipping the card into his back pocket.

"About ten years."

"After you retired?"

Swanson frowned at him. "Retired?"

Dom nodded toward the honking diamond on Swanson's right hand. Bought on eBay? "I see that Super Bowl ring on your finger. Who'd you play for?"

"The 49ers."

"Great team. Their last Super Bowl win was one of the most exciting games I've seen. Three plays and less than two minutes into the game and they'd already scored. What position d'you play?"

"Special teams."

Figured he'd pick that. Most special teams players could play ten years in the NFL in virtual anonymity. "What was your specialty?"

"Covered punts and kickoffs."

Why didn't that surprise Dom? Swanson was plain telling him he was aggressive, fast and reckless in his pursuit. A warning that he didn't care what happened to Jill? That he'd get what he wanted no matter who came after him? Kick him down, he'll just get back up again? "What's your last name again?"

"Swanson."

"Oh, yeah, I remember you. They called you Suicide Swanson." Convenient that the real Swanson—Brent, not Warren—had died not long after that Super Bowl win.

Swanson's eyebrows rose in surprise. "You know your football."

"Played three years for Texas A&M," Dom said. "Running back." *Right back at you. I'm just as tough and determined as you are.* "You had a pretty good record at stopping the return man inside his own twenty-yard line."

Swanson shifted his stance. "What happened to the fourth?"

"Fourth what?"

"Year."

"Tore both medial collateral ligaments and had to have three operations on my knees."

"Ouch. Still bother you?"

Couldn't have made the Hostage Rescue Team if it did. I'll get you, don't you worry your rotten little head about that. "Right as rain."

The boys came charging out the deck door. Brendan kicked at a soccer ball. Jeff tripped over the toe of his shoe and accidentally clipped Swanson's elbow as he tried to catch himself, sending the salmon steak Swanson was flipping flying off the monster grill.

His congenial face slid and was replaced with a mask of rage that slit his eyes and trembled through his jaw. But he regained control so fast, Dom had to wonder if he'd actually seen what he thought he'd seen.

"Hey, slow down, Jeffery," Swanson said, all warm and friendly again.

"Sorry." Jeff backed away from the grill, index finger pushing his glasses back up his nose.

"Just be more careful next time."

"Okay." Jeff nodded, seemingly frozen to the spot.

Time to let Swanson think he'd gotten one over on the redneck. Dom hadn't gotten much out of him, but he really hadn't expected to this early in the game. Good old Warren probably hadn't counted on all this family bonding time.

"Come on, sport," Dom said, ambling onto the lawn. "Let's see if we can get that soccer ball away from Brendan."

Jeff's nose wrinkled and he stifled a smile with one hand. "Brendan's good."

"Okay, then, two on one. You and me against Brendan."

Jeff laughed and tugged at Dom's hand. "This way."

Dom glanced over his shoulder, at Luci staring at him, arms crossed protectively over her chest. Her bone-deep weariness echoed in his own body. He hadn't been sleeping well either, lately. August did that to him, as he suspected it did to her. Cole charging into action one minute, dead the next. Both their lives ripped apart, the ghost of Cole still there between them, haunting.

"I HAVE AN ANNOUNCEMENT to make." Jill stood up as dinner mercifully drew at an end. The boys had left long ago and were playing in Jeff's room.

Luci tensed. This couldn't be good.

Jill held up her glass of wine. Her face flushed with happiness and her smile glittered more brilliantly than Warren's pseudo-diamond at her neck.

Luci's heart sank and her hands gripped the table-cloth tail under the table. *Oh, no, Jilly, you didn't.*

"I'm engaged! Warren asked me to marry him." Jill looked like a kid on Christmas day as she stuck out her left hand and displayed the emerald-and-diamond square-cut engagement ring that had not been on her finger five minutes ago.

A shocked silence froze everyone at the table. Warren was moving fast. Way too fast. Luci caught Dom's attention and tried to read his thoughts, but he played his part right. As if nothing were wrong and tension weren't as jagged as ice, he got up, raised his glass and toasted the couple. "Congratulations, you two. When's the big date?"

Jill hooked her fiancé's arm with one of her own and beamed up at him. Her ring caught the chandelier light and seemed to mock everyone at the table. "Two weeks from today."

Luci's dinner twisted itself in her stomach. Two weeks. Jill's birthday. Jill was still a kid when it came to birthdays. She needed cake and candles and wanted presents and balloons. Warren was going to not only steal her inheritance, but her joy, too. Luci couldn't let that happen.

Congratulate her. Play the part until you can prove Warren's rotten core. Luci fumbled for her glass and stood. Dom's hand flattened against the small of her back and steadied her. The words worked themselves up Luci's throat with false enthusiasm as she pinned on a smile. "Congratulations. When did Warren pop the question?"

Jill looked up at Warren, completely blinded by love. "A couple of days ago. He was so romantic. He got down on one knee right in the middle of the restaurant and said the most beautiful things." Tears of joy slid down her face. Luci prayed she could save Jill before they turned to tears of sorrow.

"Jillian, how could you?" Barbara wrung her napkin in her lap. "We can't get the country club on such short notice. Why the hurry?"

Jill's smile fell, then rebounded. "It's just going to be a small wedding. I thought we could have it here. We're in love. We don't want to wait. There's no reason"

Barbara threw her napkin onto the table. "No, that simply won't do."

Neil, ever the peacemaker, chimed in. "We'll work it out, poppet. Don't you worry. The important thing is Jill's happiness."

"Do you have any family, Warren?" Barbara asked. Luci could imagine the dozens of lists drawing themselves up in her mother's mind.

"No, ma'am," Warren said, and for a second he looked as young and besotted as Jill. He deserved an Emmy, if not an Oscar, for his performance. "I'm on my own."

"Then we'll have to take care of the rehearsal dinner, too." Barbara gestured at her husband. "Neil, get me my purse." She tapped a burgundy-polished fingernail against the tablecloth in Warren's directions. "How about friends? I'll need a list. Invitations have to go out on Monday."

For once, Luci was grateful for her mother's hyper organizational skills. Barbara would ask all the questions Luci longed to ask. In no time flat, her mother would have a list of Warren's business associates and friends. Luci would check out every name on Warren's list.

"We just want something small and intimate, Mom. Just you and Dad and Luci and Brendan."

"Surely Warren will want to invite at least some close friends," Luci said, salivating at the potential clues on her mother's list. "You're going to be part of our family, Warren. We'd like to meet the people who are important to you."

Warren skewered her gaze. Was that a shard of ice in his eyes? But his genial smile never faltered. "Jill and Jeff and our lives together are important to me. If she wants a small and intimate wedding, then that's what I want, too."

Jill wrinkled her nose and her eyes sparkled. "Isn't he wonderful?"

Fortunately, her mother didn't do small and intimate.

"That simply won't do," Barbara said. "Oh, Jillian, there's too much to do to pull off a proper wedding in two weeks."

Neil returned and handed Barbara her purse. "Thank you, darling." She dug out a small notebook and a pen. "What about a church?"

"We were planning on a justice of the peace."

"I'll see if Father Tim is free."

"That's a beautiful ring, Jill," Dom said. His hand stiffened at Luci's back and telegraphed a hum of anxiety. What was wrong? Something about the ring? "The emerald's green suits your eyes."

"That's what Warren says, too." Jill leaned her head against Warren's shoulder and looked up at him in complete adoration. "My ring belonged to his mother. Isn't that so sweet?"

Luci's heart ached for her sister. She wasn't going to let him walk her sister up the aisle, then stomp on her heart while he hightailed it to his next victim. She'd stop him before it got that far. A trap, that's what they had to do, set a trap. She'd have to think of something. Fast. Two weeks, that's all she had to save Jill.

Luci grasped Dom's hand, wanting desperately to ask him about the new tension thrumming beneath his easy smile since Jill had shown off her ring. With a squeeze of his fingers, he acknowledged her worry. Then he reached for the bottle of wine and refilled glasses all around. "A toast to the happy couple. May happiness follow them to the end of their days."

Luci lifted her glass. *May we stop this scam artist before he causes irreparable damage.*

Using her goats as an excuse to have to get home, Luci cut the evening short. As she and Dom followed Brendan to the van, she grabbed Dom's arm and whispered, "What's bothering you?"

"The ring." His voice was a low growl that reverberated with portent. "It belonged to Laynie McDaniels, his last victim."

WARREN WAS GLAD to get rid of the last of the unwanted guests. Keeping up appearances was getting harder with each sinner. Maybe it was time to hang it up and enjoy the spoils of his hunts. Jill's million-dollar payday would complement the rest of her portfolio rather well, thank you. He could take some time off, winter in the Caribbean or wind his way through Europe. He deserved a vacation. Christmas in Vienna sounded good. Or maybe he'd finally make his dream of sailing around the world come true. There was no way he could get to all the sinners in his lifetime, anyway.

Jill deposited the last of the wine glasses on the counter. "It went well, don't you think?"

"Splendidly, sweetheart." He sank a glass into the hot suds in the sink and sponged away the red stain at the bottom. Wiping away the stain on Jill's soul would take more than a sinkful of dishwater.

Jill fussed with the leftover rice pilaf. "Luci's worried that you want me just for my money."

"Your sister seems to carry a rather large chip on her

shoulder. Don't listen to her. I'd love you even if you didn't have a penny."

"That's what I told her."

Warren swallowed his glee at having found such an easy mark. "You saw her tonight, sweetheart. Between her and your mother, you'll be pulling your hair out by the end of the week. I think we should just go ahead and do things the way we'd planned. Sweet and simple."

Jill gave a mirthless chuckle. "You don't know my mother."

The mother he could handle. She was just a manipulative old bat and he could make her come around to seeing his way. The sister, that was something else. She'd looked at him as if he were the devil himself.

If she only knew.

Not the devil, but a savior. He would show Jill the error of her ways. He would save her from her selfish goals. The same way he'd shown the other spoiled bitches. And if she was too stupid to learn, she'd suffer Laynie's fate. At least Laynie's melodramatic personality had given him the perfect alibi. Everyone, even the police, had believed she'd hanged herself.

"Your mother is a sweetheart and wants to share in your happiness," Warren said. He placed the last glass on the dish drain, dried his hands and wrapped them around Jill's waist. "Your sister, on the other hand, is simply jealous of your good fortune."

Jill frowned and fingered the edge of his collar as if it were a security blanket. Her complete trust heightened his lust.

"I don't think she's jealous," Jill said, her voice wavering with uncertainty. "Luci isn't like that. She's just afraid I'll get hurt."

He had to use Jill's uncertainty to gain what he wanted, a separation between the sisters. The less Luci could influence Jill, the better for him. "I guess you feel frustrated by Luci's smothering."

"She means well." Jill snuggled against his chest.

"I know your ex-husband hurt you, but I'm not like him." He patted her back, encouraging her dependency. "But you have me now. I'll be a good role model for Jeff. I can take care of all those details a wonderfully alive woman like you shouldn't have to worry about. That squeaky garage door'll be gone by tomorrow. Then I'll talk to the club and see what they can do about fitting us in for a small, intimate ceremony. That should please your mother."

Jill peppered his cheek with kisses. "Oh, Warren, how did I get along without you?"

"Hey, that's what makes me such a great private detective, taking care of details. And I know what it's like to be on your own."

She leaned back, the gleam in her eyes bringing out the green flecks in the brown irises. "I love you."

"I love you, too, my heart." He kissed the tip of her nose. "I don't want to see you frown before the wedding. It's a happy time for both of us. Maybe you should give Luci some space until after the ceremony. She'll come around when she sees how happy you are."

Jill's lips curled in, the beginning of a pout. "Maybe you're right, but it's going to be hard. I wanted her to be my maid of honor."

He jostled Jill's hips, his body reacting to her welcoming curves. "Why not ask another friend, one who's as happy as you are, to support you on your special day? How about Amber? She seems nice."

"You're right. I deserve to have someone who's happy standing by my side."

"Looks much better in the photos."

"I wish Luci could see how good you are for me."

She does, you silly bitch. That's why she's so dangerous. "The sooner we're married, the sooner our happiness starts." He nuzzled Jill's neck, then pulled her toward the bedroom. Sex would keep her distracted until the ink was dry on their marriage certificate.

Chapter Six

The goats were milked and chewing contently on hay in their pen. The chickens were bedded down in their coop. Brendan was bathed, tucked in bed and asleep. Luci had stretched the busywork as far as she could and the clock showed it was nearly midnight.

Dom wasn't going to go away.

When she could no longer put off the inevitable, she reached for clean sheets in the linen closet and headed for the spare room where she unfolded the futon.

Dom stood in the doorway, leaning his big body like a roadblock across the opening, making her much too aware of him, of how easily she could let herself fall back into old patterns and seek comfort against his wide shoulder, let his smooth slow voice talk her into— what?—a relationship? She shook out the bottom sheet, snapping it. No, that was crazy. He wasn't heading there. He wanted the same thing she did: Warren behind bars.

The glow on Jill's face as she'd gazed up into Warren's eyes had stirred something inside Luci. How long had it been since she'd looked at a man with love in her eyes? Seven long years. She hadn't realized how much she'd depended on her sister for companionship these last six years until Warren had turned Jill's head so completely. But Dom was the wrong person to fill that emptiness. Leaning on him wouldn't have any happier an ending than Jill's engagement to Warren. Luci couldn't do that to herself or to Cole.

Think of Dom as nothing more than a Hostage Rescue Team member and this situation as nothing more than gathering intelligence for a mission.

Luci tucked in the top sheet, making precise military corners. "How could Warren give Jill a dead woman's ring?"

"Recycling."

She shot him a dark look. "That's not funny."

"Time was, you would've been the one to come up with the joke."

Luci sighed as she picked up a pillowcase. Time was, she would have. Black humor was a way to survive the horrors they'd often had to deal with. Not any more. When was the last time she'd laughed, truly laughed all the way down to her belly? Before Cole's death. With him and Dom in her tiny apartment in Texas after a round of miniature golf that had started as a joke and ended up as a full-out competition. Cole had won, as usual, and supplied the pizza and beer for their post-game celebration.

Fighting tears, Luci shook a pillow into the pillowcase. "I figured out where Warren found Jill."

"Where?"

Luci dropped the pillow on the bed and reached for the comforter, focusing on each movement of her task instead of the blatantly male lines of Dom's body. "She went to Florida last spring to visit a college friend. Warren must have zeroed in on her back then and spent the summer checking up on her."

"Could her friend be in on the scam, pointing out possible targets?"

Luci tried to picture ditzy Andrea D'Alessandro colluding with Warren. She supposed anything was possible, especially if Andrea's party funds were running low. That seemed unlikely when her husband could buy a small country if he wanted. "I don't know. But she makes the Miami gossip columns often enough with her party lifestyle that she might have come up on Warren's radar that way."

"I'll check if Jill's name made any of the papers during her visit."

Luci smoothed the comforter over the double bed. Dom's feet would probably hang over the end. But he was used to that, as many nights as he'd spent on her couch. She sat on the edge of the bed, hands on her thighs and forced her mind back to task. "Did things get too hot for Warren in Florida?"

Hands stuffed in his back pockets, Dom was studying her much too intently. "It's always better to leave the scene of the crime. Staying in the same place, he risks running into people he's already met. And if he's using a different name, that makes it easier to get caught in a lie. He'd want distance."

Luci nodded, focusing on Warren's movements and hoping they would lead to something they could use against him. "So he moves after every scam. Did he scam someone in Florida?"

"I haven't found any evidence. Yet. His pigeon might

be too embarrassed to have reported the swindle. Or it may simply be his base of operations."

Luci curled her fingers over the round of her knees. "He loves them, then he leaves them, broke and heartbroken. He uses their pride to make his great escape. When does he change his ID? And how?"

"He probably builds several IDs at the same time. He doesn't stay in any one of them long enough to cause a blip. Other than the fact he's swindling millions of dollars from divorced women desperate for love, he's a law-abiding citizen. Not so much as a traffic ticket in any of his IDs. It costs, but you can get new real ID."

And to get the necessary papers to build a new identity, he'd have to know low-rent contacts. "Any chance of finding out who supplies him with those papers with those Florida Social Security numbers?"

"Not until I catch him in the act."

"So another dead end." Luci grabbed one of the decorative pillows she'd dropped on the floor and hugged it. "Still, why Jill? Even with her money and her son and her divorced status, what tipped the scale in her favor rather than some other woman? He had to have dozens to pick from. Was it because she lived so far from Florida?"

"Could be. He has an affinity for boats. That's the one common denominator for each of his new destinations."

"New Hampshire doesn't have much shoreline," Luci pointed out. "And we're not anywhere near the ocean."

"But look at where Jill lives," Dom said. "Near a river. And those huge windows in her living room and kitchen made me feel as if I was right on the water."

Luci groaned. "You're right. And then there's the lake house. J.J. and Jill still share that. And the speed-boat." Luci squeezed the pillow tighter against her chest. "She fits."

"Down to the last detail."

Luci scrutinized her ragged nails against the navy blue chenille of the pillow and thought of her mother's and her sister's perfectly manicured red ovals, of the perfectly pressed gaggle of moms at Brendan's soccer games, of how perfectly ridiculous it was for her to ex-pect to fit in. And for the first time in her life, she didn't want to. Not if fitting in made her a target for some scam artist the way Jill had. "If Warren did zero in specifi-cally on Jill, then that's the criminal intent you need, right?"

"If I can prove it."

She finally dared to look into Dom's eyes. For an in-stant, the pale blue emitted tempting heat that reached down to her bones. She shook her head. Filled with new determination, she rose and tossed the decorative pil-low onto the nearby rocking chair. "Then we have to find a way to prove it. I can't let Jill marry him. And I can't ruin her happiness without proof he intended to hurt her from the get-go."

She marched toward the door and came up against the roadblock of Dom's body. He smelled like crisp night air that reminded her somehow of deep velvet and bright stars. Soap? Aftershave? It didn't matter. She didn't care. She wrapped one arm around her waist and pointed toward the kitchen. "I, uh, need to get my purse. I have Jill's account numbers. You can get them to your computer guy."

He moved, giving her plenty of space to get around him, yet air constricted in her lungs anyway as she went by. At the kitchen counter, she fumbled with the flap of her purse. "We need to come up with a plan to get into his office and his apartment. Check his computer. Anything that would prove he knew who Jill was before he bumped into her at the country club. He can't have memorized everything. There has to be *something* that'll incriminate him."

Maggie's barks ripped the night's quiet. Luci pushed aside the curtain of the window above the sink and peered into the dark yard. She couldn't see a thing. She headed toward the door, slipped into her barn clogs and reached for a flashlight on the windowsill.

"Want me to check it out?" Dom asked, moving in too close again.

"No. Maggie's probably just tangling with a skunk or bothering the goats. That dog has no common sense."

But as soon as Luci opened the back door, Maggie's barks morphed into yelps of pain. Luci hurried to the back of the barn and found the door she knew she'd closed ajar and Maggie a shaking mass of blond and brown fur with her tail tucked between her back legs.

"What's wrong, Mags?" Luci flashed the light around, but saw nothing out of sorts. No fleeing bad guy. No departing vehicle. Was someone still in the barn?

Maggie whimpered, tried to get up and fell over.

"What happened to you?" Luci patted down the mutt, looking for broken bones and found a tender spot on her ribs. "Did Faye kick you?"

Maggie flopped her head down, closed her eyes and panted.

"I've told you to stay away from her. She doesn't like to be herded, especially in the barn."

Maggie whimpered.

"Okay, let's get you inside."

Luci wrapped her arms around Maggie, but each attempt to lift her off the ground only brought a round of painful yips.

"I'll get her, " Dom said. He handed his own flashlight to Luci, then speaking low nonsense words to the dog, he lifted Maggie into his arms as if she were a baby. She licked at his face.

"I'm going to take a look around the barn," Luci said, aiming her beam at the unlatched door.

"Wait till I get back."

"I can handle it."

"That's not the point."

Maggie groaned.

"I'll be right back," Dom said.

Just as he and Maggie started heading back, a crash came from inside the house.

Brendan!

Had Maggie been a distraction? Heart beating a frantic gallop, Luci bolted inside. Out of habit she walked out of her clogs without missing a beat and darted up the stairs three by three. Flashlight aimed like a mace to pound on anyone who'd dare harm her child, she rushed into her son's room. Something hard and cold bit into the arch of her bare foot. She kicked it aside and flipped on the overhead light switch.

"Brendan?"

Brendan's dark head popped over the side of the toppled three-drawer bureau. A maze of orange Matchbox car track looped from the bureau to Brendan's bed. "I can explain."

Never a good start. Luci stepped away from the row of Matchbox car lined up along the edge of the rug. Brendan was frantically trying to right the downed bureau before he got into too much trouble.

"What happened here?" Luci asked, hand on her heart, pushing its mad beating back to normal. She bent over to help Brendan pull the bureau back in place.

"It's not my fault," Brendan said. Tears squiggled down his cheeks as he picked up a piece of broken track. "It fell over."

"I can see that. Why did it fall over? You're supposed to be in bed."

"I wanted to try a triple flip. I figured out how to do it."

Why didn't that surprise her? Cole had been filled with the same kind of restless energy. "Next time wait until morning. Or ask for help."

He pitched the piece of broken track against the wall. "It's broken."

"We'll fix it tomorrow. Now back to bed." Luci pushed aside the plastic track, tucked Brendan in and kissed him good-night for the second time, relieved that her fears of violence against him were unwarranted.

When she got to the kitchen, she found Dom hanging up the phone.

"How's Maggie?" she asked, kneeling beside the dog's beanbag bed. The skin above Maggie's eyes wrinkled in pain, but she gamely tried to wag her tail at the sound of her name.

"Broken rib, I think. I called a twenty-four hour

clinic in Nashua. I'll take her in after the police get here."

"The police?" Luci shook her head and petted Maggie's long ears. "That's not necessary. The crash was nothing. Brendan was trying to build a triple loop for his Matchbox cars and he toppled over his bureau in the process."

Dom's silence hung heavily in the air, forcing her to look up. She hadn't seen Dom's face so tense since the day she'd told him she never wanted to see him again.

"Someone killed your chickens," he said.

Her heart kicked into high gear and her fingers shook against Maggie's coat.

"Someone? You mean an animal?" She'd spotted a fox just the other day, hanging out at the edge of the woods that bordered her property. That's why she made sure to bring in the chickens before dark. But even before Dom answered, adrenaline scrambled her pulse.

"Not unless he carries a wire garrote."

DOM STARED at the row of chickens strung up from the rafter the way Laynie McDaniels had been hanged with her own belt in that motel closet. Was Swanson hoping the slaughter would distract Luci from worrying about her sister's upcoming wedding? Or was it a threat?

Jill's assets were at stake, but now so might Luci's life if she caused Swanson too much grief.

Dom unhooked the last hen from her wire noose and gently lay her body in the wheelbarrow. Luci didn't need to deal with this massacre. Brendan certainly didn't need to witness it.

When and how had Swanson managed the feat? The

chickens were still alive when they'd gotten home and taken care of the evening chores. Why hadn't the chickens panicked at the invasion of their coop? Even Maggie hadn't noticed the intrusion until it was over. Not that she was much of a guard dog. She'd never barked at him, not even when he'd been a stranger to her.

Dom had walked every inch of the yard. The only thing out of place was that the coop and barn doors were left ajar. He searched for tire tracks along the shoulder of the road in front of Luci's farm, but the hard-packed ground had given up nothing. Dusting for prints would gain him nothing, not on this rough wood surface. He'd bet the wire cutters were Luci's and wiped clean. Swanson was an expert at disappearing without leaving much of a trace. Especially with so much money and a jail sentence at stake. He'd send the wire cutters in for testing anyway.

Dom wheeled the dead chickens to the edge of the woods and shoveled at the hard, granite-seeded earth. Wind howled through the trees like a child in pain, the threat of rain riding on its gusts. The cold lash of it whipped at his face and through the thin material of his shirt.

The two drive-through cheeseburgers and the milkshake he'd downed on his way back from the veterinary clinic with Maggie while Luci dealt with the police hadn't done a thing to stanch the gnawing of anxiety fueling his body. Neither had the hard work of digging a grave.

He shouldn't have come here. He shouldn't have involved Luci. He should have found some other way to get to Swanson. He'd thought he could handle being around Luci again. He hadn't counted on the memories.

On having her eyes silently plead with him tonight as they had after Cole's fall. On her becoming a threat to Swanson.

An internal investigation cleared the team of wrong-doing after Cole's death. But Dom should have realized much sooner that the situation was unstable, that words weren't going to help.

"Let someone else step in, Skyralov," the Special Operations Group leader had suggested.

"No, I've got a rapport going. I just need a bit more time." If the assault team charged, someone would get hurt—most likely the kid.

"What's going on? Why'd you stop talking?" Grigsby asked, agitated. *"You getting ready to shoot me?"*

"I needed some water," Dom said into the phone. *"Nobody's going to shoot anybody. We all want everyone to walk out of this alive."*

"I need money. I need transport. Now."

"And I'm willing to get those for you, but I need you to give me something in return. I'll trade you the boy for the chopper you want."

"Screw it. Get me money. Get me wheels. Then we'll talk."

Grigsby slammed the phone.

"Anyone got a fix on him?" Dom said into the mic.

Luci whispered, seemingly right into his ear, "He's still got the kid strapped to him. He's pacing like a boar about to charge and snorting some sort of powder."

Dom took in a calming breath and dialed Grigsby's number. The phone at the other end rang twenty straight times. "Come on, Joe Bob, answer."

All he got was more ringing.

Then the phone crashed through the window, shattering his last chance to end the situation peacefully.

Instead of saving two lives, he'd lost three. Four, if he counted how the light had gone out of Luci's life.

Such a waste. Cole. Luci. The chickens. All of it. And this, he thought, as he pitched another shovelful full of dirt on the growing mound at his side, was a waste, too. His mother would have a fit if she knew he was burying a dozen healthy chickens instead of harvesting their meat. But he didn't want their frozen carcasses to remind Luci of their murder long after he'd left. He'd already saddled her with enough haunting memories.

He lay the hens in the grave, then covered them with earth.

She'd warned him, hadn't she? *You are* not *bringing trouble here. Do you hear? You are* not *bringing trouble to this family. You are* not *bringing trouble to this community.* And he'd gone and done all three.

He wished he'd never met Luci. Never met Cole. Never taken the phone that day.

With the back of the shovel, he patted the last of the dirt onto the grave, then headed to the coop. He scrubbed every inch of the small building until someone could have eaten off the floor, then readied the nests for their next occupants.

By the time he headed back to the house, dawn was pushing at the horizon, sweat streaked his shirt and he'd come up with no good answer to his dilemma. If he told Luci to back off, she'd push forward—especially with the wedding less than two weeks away. Having Falconer send someone else would mean taking time they didn't have to bring another Seeker up to date, work up another cover that couldn't be as efficient as Dom's and give Swanson the chance to slip away yet again.

The best way to protect Luci was to stay close.

As he pushed through the back door of her home, the scent of bacon, eggs and blueberry muffins greeted him. Luci stood at the stove, her braid like a pendulum swinging gently across the back of her faded blue sweatshirt as she stirred the eggs. He wanted to run his hand down the rope of hair, tickle his palm with the ends. Instead, he soaped his hands at the sink and tried to wash away his need to hold her.

Without turning to face him, Luci said, "You didn't have to take care of the chickens."

"I didn't want Brendan to see them."

Her throat worked hard and her voice was hoarse. "Thank you."

After he dried his hands, she passed him a plate heaping with food and he tucked into it as if he hadn't eaten in a week. As good as breakfast was, it did nothing to slow the inner corrosion eating him alive.

She sat at the opposite end of the table, nursing a cup of coffee. Had she slept at all? He doubted it. Fatigue drooped her eyes, rimming the delicate skin below with dark purple moons. How long since she'd had a good night's sleep?

"I'll take care of the goats this morning," Dom said, reaching for a muffin. "You get some rest."

"Brendan'll be up soon."

"He can help me in the barn."

Her fierce grip around the white mug squeezed the blood from her fingers. "We need to talk about a plan to get into Warren's office and apartment."

"There's time."

"No, there isn't." One finger drilled the tabletop in time to the anger she worked hard to suppress. "Didn't you hear him last night? In two weeks, he'll marry Jill. How long do you think it'll be before he disappears and leaves her in a mess?"

"You're dead tired, Luce." Pushed away his empty plate, but restlessness still ate at him. "We'll talk about it after you get some rest."

"I'm fine. This is normal for me."

No, this wasn't normal. Normal was a smile that dazzled and green eyes that lit up like a Christmas tree. Normal was taking on the dare of a miniature golf round with all the seriousness of a PGA event and making it fun. Normal was being part of the Hostage Rescue Team and fitting in like one of the guys.

His gaze found hers and met pure determination. At least one thing was still there—her loyalty. She would do whatever it took to keep those she loved safe, even at the cost of her own well-being.

Dom could do this. He could sit near her, discuss a case like they used to and pretend, as he'd done then, that his feelings for her were nothing more than brotherly. Always before, his training had allowed him to compartmentalize, lock his feelings in a box and do the job. He was the patient man, the calm, cool one.

He got up, grabbed a cup down from the doorless cupboard and filled it with coffee. He hated coffee, but Luci didn't seem to have green tea and he'd need the caffeine to get through the day. "You should let me take care of Swanson alone."

"You're the one who asked for my help," she snapped.

"I didn't know how much it was going to take out of you."

"I've gone through worse." She shook her head and her mouth turned up in a half sneer. "I'm a survivor."

"That's a cop-out and you know it. Surviving isn't living." Dom used the refrigerator door as armor and sought milk for his coffee. "We need to talk about him." How did he expect Luci to bring up the ghost between them, if he couldn't speak his name? "We need to talk about Cole."

The refrigerator's motor kicked on in a low growl.

Luci's fingertips reddened against the white mug. "Cole has nothing to do with Jill."

"But he has everything to do with you." *And us.* Dom didn't want to feel guilty for the rest of his life. And this, he suddenly realized, was why he'd broken his vow to Luci. He wanted to confess his sins, let daylight purge them.

He wanted her forgiveness.

In the thickness of the tension, his pulse pounded past his ears like a hammer. The breakfast he'd inhaled turned to rock.

Luci stared at him for what seemed an eternity. "Luci? Are you okay?"

She blinked once, slowly. As if he'd punched her, she rose, using the table for support. Then, back straight, legs stiff, arms determined pistons, she tore upstairs never looking back at the monster who'd pried open the box of her grief.

Chapter Seven

Luci couldn't talk about Cole. She couldn't admit her guilt, couldn't face the darkness of her failure, of Cole's blood on the floor, of his vacant gaze staring back at her. By default, she took Dom up on his offer to watch over Brendan. Shaking with a cold that had nothing to do with the autumn weather, she fell into bed and curled into a fetal position. She spent the morning sewing up the edges made raw by remorse.

Her guilt was a burden she couldn't ask Dom to carry. His eyes were already too weighted with sadness. Cole's death had left scars on his heart, too. She'd already asked too much of him after Cole's death.

Instead, she should look to his example. He hadn't hidden himself as she had. He'd kept doing what was important to him. And throughout everything, he'd kept his optimism and remained self-assured. He still made things happen. He still could dream. That strength of character had made her turn to him early on during training, and kept her turning to him for support.

Now, more than ever, she had to stand on her own two feet.

She squeezed her eyes shut and started folding the corners of memories into ever-smaller pieces.

By lunch, rain lashed at the windows. Arms wrapped tightly around her knees, she sat and watched the sky cry the tears that wouldn't come, fill the emptiness yawning inside her.

By dinner, she'd put herself and a chevron stew together and was ready to deal with Dom once more. He was trying to save Jill and put Warren behind bars. She wasn't going to burden him with her baggage. Nor would she let her weakness become a liability to him. She'd been strong once. She could be so again. For Jill. And getting Warren in a place where he couldn't ever hurt someone like Jill again was the important thing right now.

After she put Brendan to bed, she cornered Dom in the living room. He was using her computer, his big body bent over the small desk as if it were made for a dwarf. The mock tiffany lamp gave his skin a warm glow and highlighted the gentle lines bracketing his eyes and mouth like a permanent smile.

She wasn't used to having another adult—a man—sharing her space. She should say something, apologize for her earlier behavior, but all she could do was stare at him and wonder why seeing him there felt so right.

"It's your house, Luce," he said without turning around. "You don't have to tiptoe around me."

"I, uh, we need to talk. About Warren."

He swiveled in the chair, his gaze locking with hers. "The chickens were a warning for you to stay out of this."

"You think he knows you're after him?"

"I think he sees your protectiveness of Jill as a threat."

Luci had given up everything about her old life with the team in order to give Brendan the security of family and small-town life. She might have let a lot of instincts go dormant, but protecting what was hers wasn't one of them. "That's not going to change."

"You have to make him think it has, or it might cost you your life." The softness of Dom's voice masked his words' sting. "Brendan depends on you."

The sharpness didn't register until after the blade had cut, slicing directly into her gut. "That's hitting below the belt."

"That's taking every contingency into consideration. I can't risk your getting hurt."

Blowing out stale air, she dropped onto the overstuffed couch and clasped her hands together over her knees. Her gaze focused on the amoeba-shaped stain on her jeans as her mind whirled. "I thought that if I came home, if I made my world smaller, I could keep it safe, keep Brendan safe."

The chair protested as Dom rose. He crouched next to her. Fingers of one hand folded around her chin, he gently turned it until their gazes met. The warmth of his enveloping hand, of his comforting blue eyes, of his calming voice, oddly made her shiver.

"How often did hostage situations follow a script?" he asked.

"Never." She shook her head, her heart ripping in two. "I can't watch Warren tear Jill apart. I can't hurt Brendan, either."

"Let me handle it. I owe you that much." He combed

his fingers through her hair and she closed her eyes against the need to lean into the support of his touch.

"You don't owe me anything." With regret, she pulled her head out of his warm connection. "And I can't let you take on the load yourself. Isn't that the strength of a team? Numbers?"

Dom didn't answer right away. The stirring in his eyes betrayed the keen blade of his evaluation of her. "A team is only as strong as its weakest member. It's been years since you trained. Skills go soft without practice."

"I can do this. I can make Warren believe I've changed my mind."

Dom rocked back on his heels and said nothing.

"I'm as good as anyone on the team ever was," she said and couldn't help the note of challenge in her voice. "And you don't need a sniper, Dom, you need Jill's sister." Luci stood up. "Tomorrow morning, I'm going to call my mother and we'll get involved with planning Jill's wedding. That'll give us a reason to go over to Warren's office and look things over. In the meantime, I want to see everything in your file on Warren. If I go through it again, I might see something I missed the first time."

For the first time in a long while, the stir of something waking deep inside her fluttered alive. She'd loved the team. She'd loved saving lives. She'd loved knowing her special skill could make a difference.

Or destroy her world.

"So what time does an insurance salesman go to lunch?" she asked.

Dom's smile canted up slowly, reaching all the

way up to his eyes, making them glitter with humor that caused her to feel lighter. He slouched in that sexy way of his, compelling someone unaware of his lethal skill to believe they had nothing to fear from him. He deepened his drawl, letting its smoothness reverberate like a caress. "Well, considering I'm working on making my hours my own, anytime you want, darlin'."

"Then it's a date."

"WE'RE HERE TO OBSERVE," Dom warned her as Luci parked her van on Main Street in Nashua.

"I know," Luci said, but the thought of finally *doing* something had her pulse hopping with anticipation. "Gathering intelligence. I've done this a time or two."

"Not recently. If you don't calm down, your pulse rate is going to give you away."

"Right." She took a deep breath in and shouldered the strap of her purse.

"Smile and remember to relax, as if you truly want him to become part of your family."

"Right." Luci reached for the door handle and got out of the van.

"Mirror and echo," Dom said as he joined her on the sidewalk.

She looked up at him and gave him her most confident smile. "Dom…"

Twin flames smoldered in the blue of his eyes before he quickly doused their heat. "What?"

"I know how to do this." She stuffed quarters into the meter.

"Right." He stuck both hands in the front pockets

of his dress pants as his long, easy stride ate up the sidewalk.

"I need to keep an eye on the clock. I have to head back by two so I can pick up Brendan at school."

"We'll make it with plenty of time."

She hooked a hand around his elbow and instantly regretted her attempt to play her role of girlfriend. Continuing the movement and putting her head on his shoulder would be so easy…so natural. And the last thing she needed to do was mix up playacting for the real thing just because she was missing Cole and Dom was conveniently there.

"The goal is to take everything in," Dom said, his voice skimming over her skin as tenderly as a kiss. "Later we'll play what's-wrong-with-this-picture."

They crossed the street and headed for the address on the card Warren had given Dom. The building was a narrow, turn-of-the-century, three-story, red brick box. The glass doors opened to a lobby with dim light. Twelve mailboxes lined one wall and a black board with white lettering announced the tenants. Warren was on the second floor. No elevators here, just creaky steps whose squeaks echoed as loudly as a radio theater's sound effect.

Jill was right. Warren had done everything he could to turn his office into something that could have come out of an old black-and-white detective movie. The door had frosted glass and gold-and-black lettering. Luci opened the door and walked into an office set up with an antique desk and old-fashioned file cabinets. Three framed certificates hung on the wall. A lone plant filled the corner.

Warren rose from behind his desk at their entrance. "Luci, Dom, how nice to see you."

"Hi, Warren," Luci said, offering her hand. Warren wore a dark suit and a white shirt that showed off his perfect tan. Was it the spray-on kind newly available at a nearby tanning salon? "Dom's taking me out to lunch, so I thought I'd save Mom the trouble of coming into town for your guest list."

"Yes, Barbara phoned." Though Warren smiled, he didn't sound too pleased.

Too bad her mother's call had taken away the edge of surprise. Had Warren had time to hide any incriminating evidence? "Oh, good, so it's ready. Join us for lunch, then."

"I'm busy on a case right now. No time for either task, I'm afraid. I want to have all my ducks lined up so I can take time off for Jill's and my honeymoon."

Luci made her face light up with pleasure. "Oh, you've decided where you're going to go?"

"Paris." He smiled. The man was definitely good-looking. He had the kind of face a camera would love—and she dearly wanted his next photo to be a mug shot. "Jill thinks it will be romantic."

Jill would. Too bad it probably wasn't going to happen. Not with Warren, anyway. "She's wanted to go there since she read the Madeline books as a kid."

Dom grunted as if he were a backwoods moose. "You'll earn some major husband points there."

"Are you sure you can't join us for lunch?" Luci asked. "We can work on your list while we eat."

"I'm afraid this isn't a good time."

Stay open and friendly, Luci. "You have to eat."

"Come on, Luci, give the man a break," Dom said, and loosely strung his arm around her shoulder. "He's trying to clear his desk for his honeymoon."

Luci pouted. "Mom's going to be upset if I don't come back with that list. She's adamant that the invitations go out today." Luci fished in her purse and brought out the sample she'd borrowed from her mother. The edge was trimmed with silver and a satin ribbon held on the vellum overlay. "What do you think? Pretty classy for homemade on the computer. Jeff showed his grandmother how to make them."

"Your mother has good taste." Warren handed her back the invitation. "You've had a change of heart about me since Saturday?"

Luci spread her palms up in an open gesture. "Jill's happy. How can I not be happy for her?" She slanted Warren a sheepish look. "Dom pointed out that perhaps I was being a bit too overprotective. I'm sorry about that."

Warren hitched the side of his pants, perched on the corner of his desk and cocked his head. "Apology accepted. Jill's lucky to have a sister who cares so much about her."

Luci jerked one shoulder and mirrored his head tilt. "Thanks for being so understanding." She planted herself into one of the two wooden chairs in front of Warren's desk. "Actually, I did have an ulterior motive for coming to see you today. I want to hire you."

Warren frowned. "Have you misplaced someone?"

Cole's image flashed in her mind, temporarily sidetracking her. She shook her head and made it look like a no. She could control her mind. "Someone killed my chickens Saturday night. The police say there's nothing much they can do about it. They think it's just kids playing a prank. Who would do such a cruel thing as a prank? I'd like to find whoever did that and at least have them replace the chickens."

Dom squeezed her shoulder. "The last thing Warren needs right now is another case. He's trying to clear his desk for his honeymoon."

Warren shook his head and took a seat behind his desk. "No, that's all right. Luci's going to be my sister-in-law. I'll see if I can come up with anything."

"Thank you. It'll be nice having a private eye in the family."

Warren pulled open a drawer, drew out a pad of yellow paper and poised his pen over the paper. "Do you have any suspects?"

"I can't think of anyone that would do such a cruel thing."

"Have you seen any strangers hanging around your property?"

Luci pressed her lips in thought. "No. I sell my extra eggs, but I leave them by the fence in a cooler. Only people who live on my road would know about the eggs."

"Random acts of violence are hard to solve unless the victim knows the perpetrator. Usually, I find that it's someone close. Tell you what. You work on a list of possible suspects and I'll work on a list of guests for your mother. I'll drop by after work and take a look around, if that works for you."

She hugged her purse. "That would be great."

"Come on, Luce, let's leave the man alone." Dom gestured grandly toward the door.

"Just a couple of names will keep Mom happy." Luci rounded up the friendliest smile she could muster.

"I have to look up the addresses."

"Okay, then." Luci shouldered her purse as she stood. "Be warned that my mother lets nothing get in the way of her party planning. It's much easier to give her what she wants."

Warren gently shepherded them toward the door. "The last thing I want is to earn your mother's wrath."

WELL, WELL, Warren thought as he watched Dom and Luci stride down the street and enter a bistro three doors down. Dom's hand spanned Luci's back protectively, guiding her like someone closer than a simple friend. The attraction seemed real enough, but a bad feeling coiled in his gut. And he'd learned to heed those feelings. Listening to them had saved his butt more than once.

The last thing he needed was a protective sister meddling in his business. He'd thought the chickens would keep her busy for a while longer, but she'd turned the tables on him and assigned him to follow up on his own actions. Good thing he could control the output of that investigation.

He needed to close Jill off from her family for the next few weeks. The mother he could keep busy with the planning for the reception. But invitations weren't going to keep Luci busy for long. She needed something else, something more, something bigger. He tapped his teeth with the cap of his gold pen.

She loved her little farm and seemed attached to that big oaf of a man who'd taken up residence in her guest room.

That was the answer, of course.

What Warren did was to save kids like Jeff. Young boys shouldn't have to grow up shoved aside while their mothers panted after men. They needed their mothers' full attention and resources.

All he was doing was reminding those foolish women where their priorities should lie.

He'd love to grab and leave right now, but Jill had a big payday coming. If he could hang on for two more weeks—until their marriage certificate was signed—he could teach Jill, and her sister, a real lesson.

DOM PULLED LUCI next to him as they exited Warren's building and stepped onto the sidewalk. The accidental bump of her hip against his triggered both guilty pleasure and rightful punishment. He couldn't help wanting her. She'd gotten under his skin the moment she'd walked into that first training class twelve years ago. But his mishandling of the situation seven years ago had wiped the joy from her eyes—from her soul. She deserved better than a constant reminder of her darkest moment.

He slung an arm over her shoulder, deepening his torment. He could pretend she was just a member of the team if it killed him. As he leaned his head to whisper in her ear, her scent of peppermint and herbs teased him, made him hungry for a taste of her warm skin. "Swanson's watching."

As Dom had expected, Luci stiffened, then forced her shoulders to relax. "Do you think he's buying your performance?"

Dom's cheek twitched with the exaggeration of a

smile. "Only as long as you don't act like I'm poison ivy. Let's go in here." He led her into the bistro three doors down from Swanson's office.

"The memory game?" she asked, stepping toward the restaurant's glass door.

He nodded, holding the door open. Normal teamwork, planning strategy, closing a case. He could do normal. "I also want to see if Kingsley's gadgets are working."

"Kingsley?"

"Seekers' computer guru. Did you notice the locksmith van parked on the street?"

She nodded. "White with red lettering."

"It's listening in to Swanson's conversations. There's a small camera in the light fixture in front of his office that shows us who's coming in and going out."

"And?" she prodded.

"So far nothing on both counts."

"For a guy working on clearing cases, isn't that strange?"

"My thoughts exactly."

The sign on the hostess's stand told them to seat themselves. They took a booth in front of the window that overlooked the entrance to Swanson's office building. Dom graciously allowed her the prime perch with back to wall.

Old habits died hard. Nice to see that Luci hadn't lost them all.

They both assessed the rest of the patrons. Of the eighteen-odd tables, couples occupied only two others: two women engaged in a meal of juicy gossip and an older pair dined in companionable silence. A lone man sat near the back, concentrating on his laptop as he ate the bare-bones meal on his plate.

The decor was stark—all straight lines, sharp angles and funneled light. Dom much preferred cozy and lived-in—like Luci's house.

A waiter, as stiff as the polished aluminum wall sculpture behind Luci, handed them menus and listed the specials. Dom ordered the first thing that caught his attention, then turned back to Luci. "Do you have any paper in your bag?"

She extracted a small notebook and tore off a few pages. More digging brought out two pens.

Dom poised his pen over the scrap of paper. "Write down everything you saw."

Only the tip of her tongue showed between her teeth as she bent over the task with concentration. He cupped a hand over his forehead, blocking her out of his sight. Too distracting.

Five minutes later, their drinks—hot tea for him, iced tea for her—had appeared and their lists were complete.

"What do you think?" Dom asked as they swapped lists. He liked the boldness of her handwriting, the surety of her hand over the paper.

Luci's tongue poked the inside of her cheek as she mulled over her answer. "Do you think the degree on his wall is real?"

"Doubt it. I'll have Kingsley check. The P.I.'s license is, though. Kingsley confirmed that earlier this morning. I'll see if he can pull the application."

Luci added two packets of sugar to her tea and stirred with more vigor than needed. "But Warren's only been in New Hampshire for a couple of weeks."

"You don't have to be a New Hampshire resident to get a New Hampshire private detective license. You don't even have to be a U.S. citizen."

"Really? But don't they do a background check?"

Dom freed the fork, knife and spoon from their napkin mummy. "Sure. On the name he gave them and that would come up clean. Even if he'd used his real name, it probably would have come clean. He's never been convicted for his crimes."

"Still, there are work requirements. How could he build the experience and be out working his scams at the same time?"

Her fingers scratched at the pale blue of the tablecloth and he wanted to dome his hand over them, calm their nervous scrabbling. She'd had the steadiest hands of the team, never missed a target. And that consistent reliability had balanced the whole team.

"Same way he gets his IDs," Dom said, contenting himself with the warmth of the tea. "Pay for it."

"That's fraud, isn't it? Can't you get him on that?"

"If we can prove it." Dom bit into one of the prissy breadsticks from the long, thin basket. The tasteless paper only made him more ravenous.

Luci groaned. "It all comes back to that proof."

Yeah, just a little thing like evidence that would hold up in court. Dom flexed his fingers, breaking the breadstick he plucked from the basket. Getting his hands on something that could nail Swanson dogged him 24/7.

The waiter arrived with their food.

"I noticed a firearms proficiency certificate." Luci frowned into her Tex-Mex salad, picking at the black beans, chunks of tomatoes and corn with her fork. "Doesn't the state fingerprint for that?"

"Two sets."

"Can't we use the fingerprints to corner him? If the fingerprints from whatever name he used with his last mark match the ones when he's using Warren Swanson, then that's proof of fraud."

Dom dug into the grilled tuna, wild rice and green beans and tried to ignore the spike of stomach-eating acid ravaging his gut. "We're going for the whole enchilada. We could get him on lesser charges for obtaining a firearm under an assumed name, but it's his first offense and he'd probably walk with a slap on the wrist."

And the last thing he wanted was to give Swanson the option to roaming the country again, looking for an easy mark. Just like his brother's killer had, even though Nate was the son of a sheriff and had lost his life. His father had spent the rest of his career trying to nail Nate's two-bit dealer. All the scumbag had to do was avoid plying his street-corner heroin trade in Lamar Skyralov's territory. Not big enough fish for anyone else to care about gutting.

The low blur of background music filled the void growing between them. Luci's gaze scanned the street outside the window.

Dom finished off the last of the food on his plate, looking for more. "My guess is that in the past six months, he's been building a couple of IDs. That's why I kept losing him."

"Isn't using two IDs at the same time in the same place risky?"

"Only if he gets caught. He's been playing this game

for a long time. He's found a routine that works." One that kept him flying low enough under the radar not to attract unwanted attention.

"So maybe there was no con going on in Florida," Luci said, twirling her glass in a precise circle. "Just a fishing expedition."

"Could be." Jill's open personality had all but invited the shark in. Swanson must've thanked his lucky stars when he spotted her. Easy on the eye, a heart the size of a house and a desperate need for love.

"Did he make side trips to Florida in between his other scams?" The rolling brook of Luci's voice shook Dom out of his musings.

"Hard to tell. I've only been following him for six months. The last scam he pulled was on Laynie Mc-Daniels. The others I've been able to track down only tell me what he did to his marks, not what route he took after he left."

He snatched the last breadstick from the basket and bit down on it.

"The money," Luci asked. "Where does it go?"

"Offshore." In neat accounts no one could touch.

"Figures."

"You going to eat that?" Dom pointed at the salad she'd barely touched. She slid it across the table.

He dug his fork into the greens. "Even con men have roots. It's human nature to want to touch base with home. Maybe there's someone in Florida he goes back to."

"How can we find out?" Then a slow smile lifted the fog of sadness across her face. "The van?"

He shrugged. "If he makes a call that seems interesting, we can get a warrant to look at his outgoing calls."

But she ignored his caution and grabbed on to the tenuous bit of hope he'd offered her. "And the number could lead us to proof."

"Getting anything that way's a long shot. He's too careful."

"It's better than just sitting around waiting."

Dom slanted his head, gazed into Luci's keen eyes, lingered a little too long on the sexy pout of her mouth. "You used to be good at waiting."

Sniping required painstaking discipline to move at a snail's pace, sneak up on a target and set up a shot. Yet each of those moves required a complex thought process, refined motor skills and the kind of confidence that others mistook as arrogance. The waiting had purpose.

All *this* waiting managed to do was flail anxiety until it became a living thing with insatiable hunger.

"Yeah, well a lot of things have changed in the past seven years," Luci said with a sigh. She held up a hand blocking whatever he might have said. "I'm dealing with Cole the best I can. I don't want to talk about him."

"I'm not going to push." Though he wanted to.

"Since when?"

"Since I see how much you still hurt." He'd give her whatever she needed, even if it meant he'd have to bear the weight of his guilt for the rest of his life.

With a jerk of her chin, she pointed in the direction of his pocket, neatly detouring around the minefield she'd unwittingly created. "Go ahead. Show me how your gadget works."

"It's a tracking device I tagged on to Swanson's car." Dom flipped open his PDA. He selected the computer function and showed her the screen. "The flashing dot here tells me I'm receiving the signal. If his car moves, this will beep at me and I'll know he's on the move."

"And be able to follow him since your office is only a few doors down."

Dom nodded as he flipped closed his PDA. "That's the idea."

She took a long pull from her iced tea. "What didn't you see in Warren's office?"

Dom brought back to mind the surgical precision of Swanson's office. Everything there to create a mood, a thin veneer to hide the truth. "Paper. If he's working on a case, as he said, there'd be paper around. For all that's done on the computer, clients still like hard copies."

"Especially lawyers." Luci flicked her braid over her shoulder and skated her fingertips on the sweating glass of tea. For a moment, he was lost in the spell of the design those nimble fingers created. "What do you suppose he has hidden in the safe behind his desk?"

The black metal brute with the shiny brass handle was too Hollywood to hide anything of value. "I'd bet nothing of importance. It's all for show."

"You're probably right." Condensation oozed from between her fingers against the glass. "What about security? How hard would it be to get into his office after he's left?"

"The locks and cameras are easy enough to get around." That alone was enough to convince him Swanson kept no trace of his intention in his office. Dom narrowed his gaze at her. "But neither of us are going to go inside."

Her spine straightened with righteous indignation. "Why not? We need the proof."

"I want to avoid illegal search and entry, if possible. I don't want to taint any of the evidence we find."

Luci arched two perfect brows. "I need to go through your file on him. There has to be something we missed."

Attention to details. That's what closed a case. Fresh eyes wouldn't hurt anything.

"I'll bring it home tonight." Knives of tension cut through his gut, inflaming his already hyper digestion. He reached for the elf-size cup of green tea and found it empty. Home. He hadn't had a real one in years.

Dom glanced at his watch and signaled the waiter for the check. "Speaking of shows. I've got to get back to the office. Walk me down?"

After he paid the tab, they walked in silence, side by side, taking in the quaint atmosphere of a downtown that had had cosmetic surgery done and wanted to show off its new face. He stopped in front of brass plaque on the yellow brick facade announcing Holliday & Houghlin. He turned toward Luci and used saying goodbye as an excuse to scan Swanson's office. The light was still on, but Dom couldn't see inside this far out.

Then he made the mistake of looking into her green eyes, so full of wariness and sadness. He couldn't help himself. He tipped his head forward and kissed her.

He'd meant to keep it friendly, reassuring. But the punch of that first meeting of lips kicked through him like a mule, nearly knocking him on his butt. The taste of her exploded in his mouth. Sweetened tea and cumin and something headier than the oldest of whiskeys shot into his blood and sizzled through every cell in his body.

"For looks," he said, pushing away, trying to tame the

unleashing of years of yearning. That small taste only left him desperate for more.

"Right, okay." Heat rushed up her neck. Her gaze focused on everything but his face, which was probably just as well. This kiss, this breach of propriety, was something else they probably shouldn't talk about. He had no explanation for his action.

She lifted an arm and pointed vaguely in the direction of her van. "Well, I'd better go. Brendan's due out of school soon and I, uh, need to make a delivery before I pick him up."

How many times was she going to have to run from him as if he were a curse before he finally had the courage to take back his heart?

Chapter Eight

Dom's unexpected kiss burned on her lips all the way to the Marston Country Club. Breezing through a yellow light, Luci shook her head. Dom, of all people. He couldn't affect her that way. A kiss from him shouldn't sear. It shouldn't catch her pulse and send it racing. It shouldn't leave behind a craving for more. He was a friend. A shoulder she'd cried on. The one person who'd seen her bare soul.

He'd been Cole's best friend.

She couldn't betray her husband's trust. Not like this.

"Get real, Luci," she told her reflection in the rear-view mirror.

Dom wasn't here to seduce her. He was here to catch a scam artist and make sure the only thing he could ever get his hands on was the inside of a jail cell.

She drove past the front semicircle and around to the back of the fieldstone-and-wood building. She shoved the van into Park and pushed Dom's kiss resolutely to the back of his mind. The kiss didn't mean anything. Jill's situation had unbalanced her. She was letting her good memories of the team highlight a touch of loneliness. And Dom was there to suffer the consequence of her weakness.

Luci yanked open the minivan's back door and grabbed the cooler of greens and herbs she'd harvested that morning, the basket of lemon-rosemary dressing she'd whipped up last night and the round of goat cheese the chef had requested.

As she struggled with the delivery entrance door, a bottle of dressing rolled out of the basket and burst on the concrete, staining her black pants. "Great."

She settled her account, then went around the corner to use the employees' restroom to rinse off as much of the oil as she could from her pants. As she walked by the kitchen, the workers' conversation stopped her cold.

"Did you hear?" Luci heard one of the line cooks ask. The chopping on the cutting board added urgency to her words. "She's shacking up with an old college friend."

"You're kidding?" another answered. "Luci Taylor?"

"No, not kidding. Someone said that he's a loser, leeching off Luci because he's got nowhere else to go."

"Why's she letting him get away with that? I thought she was smarter."

"Lonely, I guess."

Luci didn't bother to stay for any more rotten raisins to drop from the grapevine. Who had started that vile rumor? Sally Kennison? Why? Not that it mattered. None of it was true. The last thing Dom was was desperate. He'd actually be pleased to know his ruse of dumb redneck was working. Still, a bitter malaise lodged in her solar plexus, radiating like acid reflux up her esophagus.

She glanced at her watch. She had five minutes left to put on her mom-face and pick up Brendan at school. What day was today? Monday? Was that a soccer practice day? She needed to keep better track of her schedule. She still had breeding to arrange for the goats, quotes to get for a new brood of chickens and the gardens to tend.

As usual, Brendan was the first to burst out of the doors at the bell. His enthusiasm spilled over in a torrent of talk as if he needed to discharge all he'd dammed up during the day to make sense of it. The ride home was never silent and seeing her son so normal warmed her heart.

Once they got home, Brendan hit the ground running, managing to race a still stiff Maggie and drop half his belongings before crashing into the kitchen.

"Wash your hands and I'll get you a snack," Luci said, shooing Maggie out of the way and reaching for the cookie jar above the refrigerator.

A *pffft* noise exploded from the tap. "No fooling around, Brendan."

"I'm not!" Brendan protested. "It's the tap. It's doing it all by itself."

With a little help, I'm sure. Luci turned around, lifted the tap and was rewarded with the same raspberry of air and tiny spray of water, followed by nothing.

She didn't need this complication right now. She already had too much to worry about.

Luci stared at the waterless tap, tracking the bubble of anger inside her as it rolled and rose. She welcomed the pitch of blinding fury, welcomed its heat and fire. But as it reached her throat, it froze, keeping her prisoner yet again.

She had Brendan to think about. Seeing his mother turn into a volcano wasn't something that would make him feel safe and secure.

She snapped the tap back to its closed position. Blank. That was better. If she let the monster out, she wasn't sure she could control it. And what she needed more than anything now was control.

Lunch with Dom and the dry faucet reinforced that need.

Her safe little world was cracking apart all around her and it seemed there wasn't much she could do about it. Standing in place, she swiveled slowly, taking in the bottom half of her house. The doorless cupboards in the kitchen, the half-stripped wallpaper. Down the hallway, the worn carpet needed replacing, the wood floor beneath refinishing. The couch in the living room was a hand-me-down from her mother.

The house and everything in it was old. Something needing repair was normal, not an act of aggression aimed directly at her. Those kinds of things happened all the time around the farm. The plumbing, the wiring, the furnace were all ancient. What should surprise her was that they'd held up for so long without needing attention.

She tromped down to the basement to examine the water pump. Fiddling with the Reset button didn't bring the thing back to life.

All she'd wanted was a quiet, ordinary life. Safety and security for Brendan. A fresh start. A second chance.

But she hadn't made peace with her mistake, and it was coming back to haunt her.

She thought about calling Dom. Maybe he'd know how to repair the water pump. But the last thing she wanted was for him to start questioning her ability to help build the case against Warren. He'd already buried the dead chickens. She could deal with this crisis on her own—just as she'd dealt with facing life without Cole every day for the last seven years.

Nerves raw and exposed, she hunted down the phone book, picked a plumber from the Yellow Pages and placed a call for service.

OUT IN THE BARN later that night, Dom invited Fanny onto the milking stand. The goat jumped up and shoved her head through the stanchion to gobble up the mix of grain in a bucket on the other side. He disinfected the udder, positioned the hooded pail in place, then sat on the bench at Fanny's right side. Before he started drawing milk, he dialed Seekers and crimped his cell phone between his shoulder and ear. As the phone rang, he directed the first squirt of milk into a strip cup and examined the results for lumps, clots or stringiness that would signal a call to the vet was in order.

"Is Kingsley in?" Dom asked when Falconer answered the phone.

"It's seven-thirty. He does have a life outside Seekers." Amusement tinged Falconer's voice.

"Yeah, of course." This time of night, a sane man was home, enjoying his family, not milking goats worrying if the next act of desperation from a con man was going to hurt someone he cared for. He started milking into the pail, finding a rhythm that was strangely relaxing. "I need an update on the Swanson case."

Papers shuffled in the background. A beep, followed by some clicking keys came next. "No activity on the

Courville accounts, except by Jillian herself. Her expenses are following their usual pattern."

Swanson wasn't going to get greedy until after he had full access, but Dom would have expected him to test the borders of Jill's generosity by now. "Kingsley was going to follow up on some leads."

"He's still looking into the previous employment and character references he culled on the private detective application. The criminal justice degree is real, but its value is debatable."

"Luci checked it out. It's one of those Internet universities. No work needed. Just money." Dom wondered at the pride filling him with warmth. Luci was wasting her skills here. Surviving. Hiding. Did she even realize she was using up most of her energy on building walls of self-protection?

"But good enough to avoid suspicion," Falconer said. "We're dealing with a master here. Don't rush things. We don't want to lose him again."

Dom didn't need the reminder. "Swanson's gotten this far because his risks are calculated. But even someone like him depends on others to make his scam work. He buys his papers from someone. He befriends someone at each port of opportunity. The key to all this is in Florida."

"Got anything to back it up?"

"Mostly gut."

Falconer made a noise that could be taken a dozen different ways. "What do you need?"

A simple question with no simple answer. A part of Dom wanted to walk away from Seekers, from Swanson and all the pond scum, the way he'd walked away from the Hostage Rescue Team. He'd do anything to give Luci the peace she needed, deserved. He'd screwed up, and Luci had paid the price. But he'd left a vital part of himself behind when he'd walked away from the team. And he'd found a corner of inner quiet again with Seekers. He needed Seekers. He needed Luci. He needed her forgiveness.

"I need someone to watch the farm while I'm tracking Swanson," Dom said as he gently bumped the udder and stripped the last of the milk in the teat. "He di͏ stray out of his office, but someone messed wi͏ ͏ ͏ ͏ ͏ 's water pump."

"What makes you say that? Sh͏ ͏ ͏ ͏ in an old house."

Old, but sound. Luci had done a good job keeping up with maintenance. "The damage on the pump wire looks too fresh for something that crept up with age. The technician agrees."

Which meant Swanson had some help. Someone local or someone he'd brought with him? And why would he suddenly take on a partner?

"Bring them in to the Aerie," Falconer offered. "I'll get Liv to prepare a couple of rooms. We can keep them safe."

Dom could imagine what kind of reception that suggestion would get him. This was Luci's home, the island of serenity she'd built for herself. "Luci won't go for that. She's a stubborn woman."

"Use her son's safety to convince her."

Falconer was putting him in a spot that was too tight for comfort. "If she and Brendan disappear, Swanson'll wonder what happened to them, especially with the wedding coming up, and why. He'll bolt."

But if anything happened to Brendan, what was left of Luci would implode. And if Luci got hurt because of his choice, he'd never forgive himself.

"I'll make sure the farm is covered," Falconer said. "What time will you be heading to town in the morning?"

"Swanson usually stirs around nine."

"I'll send Reed and Harper for the first shift."

"Appreciate it."

Dom signed off and stuffed the phone in his pocket. He rested his head against Fanny's warm hide, closed his eyes and watched Cole fall, bleed, die. Not a damn thing he could do about it. Words had failed him. His best friend had died, along with two innocent hostages. The helpless feeling that had paralyzed him then crept back into his limbs. That's why he'd quit, why he'd gone for work that required him to depend mostly on his own wits, not on his words. He'd never wanted to feel that helpless again. He'd tried to make things right for Luci, but all he'd managed was to put her in the one place she so desperately wanted to avoid—square in the middle of conflict.

If he lost Swanson now, finding him again would be harder the next go round. How many others would have to suffer because of his failure?

And if Dom wasn't more vigilant, Swanson would get away with another big payday.

THE TECHNICIAN had worked a miracle and rewired and revived the water pump in a couple of hours. Warren The Worm had come and gone. He'd examined the chicken coop, asked her if she'd had any problems with neighbors or the kids in the neighborhood. He'd taken notes and made all the right noises, but hadn't offered any hope of ever finding who had killed her chickens. Was Dom right? Had Warren killed her chickens in some sort of twisted reasoning that this would keep her off his back? He hadn't provided the promised list of wedding guests, either.

Luci scoffed as she stuffed another plate in the dishwasher after dinner. Warren had refused her invitation to dinner and managed to make it sound as if he was doing *her* a favor. But Warren didn't know her mother. Barbara wasn't going to take no for an answer. She'd have that list before the night was out. And that would give Luci another clue to follow.

She'd call her mother after Brendan was in bed. Then she could start checking out Warren's friends on the Internet.

Dom was upstairs reading to Brendan—per Brendan's insistence—while Luci cleaned up the kitchen. Having someone with whom to share the chores was nice. *Don't get used to it.* Dom's presence here was temporary. Still, having someone watch her back was a security she hadn't experienced since leaving the team and it felt…good.

Almost like a real family.

Luci jostled loose the wistful thought, chucked the counter sponge in the sink, then went upstairs. As she stood outside her son's room, peeking in at Brendan snuggling up to Dom, she was very much aware of Dom's maleness, of his big body next to her son's small one, of his deep voice contrasting with Brendan's more high-pitched one, of how Brendan could easily relate to

Dom in a way he never could to her. Maggie had sandwiched herself between the guys, her shaggy head perched adoringly on Dom's knee as if she, too, enjoyed the story. And Luci found herself yearning for something…more.

Shaking her head at her foolishness, she stepped into the room. "Time for lights out."

Nothing would bring back Cole.

If she hadn't hesitated so long seven years ago, Cole would be the one sitting beside Brendan, reading him bedtime stories. Now Brendan was lapping up the unprecedented male attention too eagerly, following Dom with hero worship in his eyes.

"Aw, Mom."

"It's way past your bedtime, buddy," Luci said, picking up discarded clothes as she went.

Brendan hung on to Dom's arm as if his small weight could anchor his new friend in place. "Just one more story. Please." He dragged out the *please* for as long as he had breath.

Dom's departure would hurt. She'd never taken that into consideration when she'd invited him into their lives.

She had to hope they caught Warren soon. The sooner Dom left, the less disruption his departure would cause.

For all of them.

"Maybe tomorrow," she said, a heavy weight settling on her heart. "It's late and you have school in the morning."

Brendan grumbled for a bit longer, but gave in when Dom promised to kick around a soccer ball with him after school the next day. Maggie settled on the rug, but Luci had no doubt the dog would hop onto the bed as soon as the door was closed.

Back in the kitchen, Luci punched the coffeemaker's On button with a knuckle, then spun around to face Dom, arms crossed. Her mouth opened, but the words dammed up in her throat because seeing him at home in her kitchen brought back the breathtaking imprint of his kiss still a ghostly pulse on her lips. "You shouldn't have done that."

Dom plunked a briefcase of rich mahogany leather onto the table and sat. "Done what?"

"Promised Brendan you'd play with him."

Dom shrugged. "I don't mind. He's a great kid."

"He's getting too attached to you."

Silently Dom pushed aside a blue place mat and pulled out Warren's case file from the briefcase. As eager as she was to scour its contents and review the updates, she couldn't pull her gaze from Dom's eyes. The longing in them was so strong that its gravity pulled her closer to the table. She gripped the edge and leaned forward. "It's not fair to him, Dom. In a few weeks you'll be gone."

"It doesn't have to be that way. I live close by, Luce. I could be there for him."

The yearning in his voice was like a dagger to her gut. Her heart beat so fast, for a second she feared it would jump right out of her chest. The possibilities unfolded before her—Dom teaching Brendan to pass a football, showing Maggie a new trick, checking the oil on the van. Then the images collapsed under the crush of pain, leaving a bruising ache in her chest.

"It would be too hard." Her legs gave out and she dropped into a chair.

Dom nodded, and the blue of his eyes seemed to dull. "I understand."

Luci reached for his hand, all sinew and muscle, and covered it with her own. "Thank you. That you care means a lot."

"Right." He grabbed the edge of the file and yanked it open, dislodging her hand. "You wanted to go over this again."

She sheathed her bereft hands between her knees. "Maybe there's something we overlooked."

Putting aside her sudden regret, Luci waited patiently as Dom laid out five piles of papers. Better to concentrate on the things she could control than the ones that were nothing but useless wishes.

Seeing Jill's name on the last pile sent a shiver down her spine. Next Dom matched five photos of Warren's various incarnations with each sheet. Then the five photos of his victims. He'd added one of Warren's current role and one of Jill. Her sister's face lined up with the rest of the women Warren had hurt made the terror he could wreak seem that much more threatening and stopping him that much more urgent.

Luci scooted her chair closer to Dom's—for ease's sake, nothing else. She'd hurt him; she deserved the coolness that frosted the air between them.

"Five women, of all shapes and sizes," she said, analytically observing the dry facts in black and white laid out on the pages. "All divorced. All with a seven-year-old son. Why? Because something happened to him when he was seven? If so, what? And why is it pushing him to marry these women and steal their money?"

Dom remained silent, organizing the contents of his file, matching them to con man and victim.

She tapped each of the victims' photos in turn. "The victims live all over the country. All the better not to get caught in his life of lies. He takes all their money." She glanced at Dom as the coffeemaker's final sigh steamed. "How does he do that?"

"Liquidates the assets once he's co-owner," Dom said. "Then he transfers them to an offshore account through a web of accounts that make it hard to trace and impossible to pinpoint the final owner. It all happens in a matter of minutes."

A lifetime zapped to nothing so fast. Destroying someone's life shouldn't be that easy. "So would financial knowledge be a way to trace his origin?"

"Not unless we have more personal details," Dom said, reaching for the platter of brownies she'd taken out of the freezer after dinner.

Brain churning, Luci got up and filled her cup with coffee. "If you're going to liquidate the whole account, don't financial institutions require both signatures?"

"Not necessarily. You'd be surprised at how easy it is. All it takes is a phone call and a few key code words. Swanson would have access to all the open-sesame secrets."

She raised the cup, silently offering it to Dom. He shook his head. Free hand flat against the tabletop, she bent over Laynie's case sheet once more.

"She's the last one he left," Luci said and sipped her coffee. "His tracks are freshest there."

"I've gone over the files a thousand times." His voice rumbled with his frustration.

Typical Dom, living with a case 24/7 until it was solved. She'd seen him talk to hostage takers for hours straight, until desperate men would trust him as if he were their older brother looking out for their best interests. All the while, it was the victims that drove him past the point of endurance.

Saving lives.

That had been all of their goals that hot, humid morning in August so long ago.

The unconscious fear that had festered deep in her gut suddenly exploded. What if she couldn't save Jill the way she hadn't saved Cole? What if she missed this time, too? What if she miscalculated and Jill ended up dead?

She sat again, too aware of the cold shaking of her limbs, of the heat discharging from Dom's body, of her desire to sink into its promise of security. Of the way his unintentional breach of her personal space thawed something inside she wasn't sure should leave hibernation.

"They were all introduced to Warren by someone they trusted," Luci continued, forcing herself to focus.

Dom covered a yawn with a hand. He'd been up for more than twenty-four hours, working like a horse for most of them. He had to be tired.

"Go to bed," she said, grabbing the coffeepot. "I'll put the file away when I'm done with it."

"In a few minutes."

"I'm fine. You don't have to babysit me."

"I know. I just wish—" He shrugged, dismissing his own needs.

And the sudden urge to grant him a wish sucked in her breath. "Wish what?"

His gaze, soft and intent, took her in as if he were trying to etch her into his memory. "I wish circumstances were different." Regret rippled beneath the words.

Frowning at the hard pummel of her pulse, she turned back to the file, anchoring herself by holding its edges with both hands. "Me, too."

She reread the scant details the file provided. They were taking her nowhere, except one big circle. "I need to talk to these women."

"Why?" The brackets around his eyes and mouth became frozen and still, giving him an air as cold as the night. "They've talked to the police. They've talked to me."

"Maybe they'll tell me something they wouldn't say to an investigator." She drew in a breath and softened her voice. "They feel stupid, Dom. They know how they look to all of you. Gullible women, desperate for love. I'm one of them. I have a six-year-old boy. I'm trying to save my sister from their fate."

He didn't answer right away. He yawned and stretched his arms behind his head. But all the pretense of relaxation wasn't fooling her one bit.

"It's worth a shot," he said.

Adrenaline splashed through her system. This would lead to something. The thrill of the hunt echoed all the way to her bones—just as it had all those years ago when the team got a call-out. "Are these addresses and phone numbers current?"

"As current as the last time I talked to them."

Luci glanced at her watch. Three hours difference with the west coast. Ten o'clock here meant it was only seven o'clock there. The perfect time to catch someone at home.

Chapter Nine

The next morning, rain pelted the roof and banged at the windows with a power that rattled and deafened like a train in a tunnel. Dom had changed out of his barn clothes after helping Luci with the morning chores and had donned his respectable office suit, minus the navy jacket currently draped over a kitchen chair.

He was fiddling with the hated red power tie, waiting to make sure Luci was safely home before he left. She would take his concern as overbearing. Tough. She'd just have to deal with it. She'd dropped off Brendan at school and was now pounding through the back door, Maggie at her heels. Dog and mistress shook the rain from their coats and sought refuge in the kitchen. Maggie headed for him, tail wringing like a flag caught in a twisting wind. Luci went for the coffeepot, poured and sighed as she took the first sip.

"No wonder you don't sleep well," he said, trying to hold a wet Maggie at a distance so he wouldn't end up with damp paw prints on his dress pants. "All that caffeine jogging through your system at all hours."

"The caffeine doesn't bother me." Steam formed a mask over her face as if to couch her lie.

Did she think she could escape her nightmares by avoiding sleep? They both needed to talk about what had happened, about Cole. Whether she liked it or not, that time would come soon. "Then you can quit cold turkey right now."

"Tomorrow." Leaning her backside against the counter, she sipped and savored. "Maybe." She eyed him up and down and the vain part of him wanted to straighten out of a slouch to give her his best angle. He didn't.

"Are you off to the office?" she asked.

"Got to play the part. You'll be okay with this storm?"

A secretive smile tipped her lips. "This rain is nothing. Have you lived through a New England winter yet?"

"A couple."

Surprise jumped in her eyes. He'd taken Falconer up on his offer to join Seekers eighteen months ago. Having Luci this close and keeping his promise to stay away from her had proved a special kind of torture. And he couldn't help himself. Once in a while, he'd driven by the farm on the off chance he'd catch a glimpse of her.

"I'm going to try calling those women again," she said, no hint of possible disappointment tainting the business tone of her voice. Her gaze strayed to the clock on the stove, calculating time zones, no doubt. She'd reached two answering machines last night and a disconnected number. Her foot tapped the linoleum and he could almost hear her cursing the clock. He liked her this way, confident and determined.

"I called Mom earlier and she gave me the three names on Warren's invitation list," Luci said. "I want to see if they lead to anything."

"Call me if you hit pay dirt." Warren wasn't about to tip his hand in any way. The short lead time to the wedding and the distance of his supposed Florida friends gave him a built-in excuse for an empty groom's side at the ceremony. "I'll run down Carissa Esslinger's current information for you."

Victim number three's phone number had been disconnected.

Luci refilled her mug. "That'd be great."

A loud crack split the warm solace of the house, followed by a resounding boom. Maggie sprang toward the door and barked.

Luci plunked her coffee mug on the counter and spun to face the back door. "What was that?"

He didn't know, but his feet were already moving him in the direction of the noise before its concussion stopped shaking the house. "Stay here."

The Seekers team hadn't arrived yet, and Dom couldn't tell if the splitting rent was man-made or natural.

Luci dogged his heels, slipping and sliding in the mud-mired yard. The woman was too stubborn for her own good. He couldn't hear anything through the cacophony of rain. The power of the downpour forced him to slow his pace to keep his balance. The cold strafe of rain drove right through his clothes, chilling skin. The unavoidable pools of water seeped cold water into his shoes.

Maggie's muffled barks from inside the house reverberated with fear.

Dom put his hand back to keep Luci behind him as he rounded the barn. The scent of her peppermint-and-rosemary soap enfolded him, penetrating the rain. His compulsion to protect her, even though she could protect herself, surprised him with its strength. Wiping rain from his eyes, he peered around the corner. The wedge of woods beyond the barn appeared like black pickets in the blurring sheets of rain. And the big oak that had shaded the barn was now down.

Her breasts were pressed against his back, scrambling his thought process. "A tree. The wind must have knocked it down and crashed it onto the barn."

The oak was perched at a precarious angle along the tip of the roof. The wind gusts and slashing rain tossed the trunk back and forth like rocking knuckles, allowing its crooked branch fingers to strike the electric wire strung between the barn and the house with a discordant *plunk, plunk.*

Luci assessed the situation and started for the barn. "Go call the power company. I'll get the goats out of the barn."

But before she could rescue the goats, the gray finger branches snapped the wire, allowing the trunk to roll right onto the power box attached to the barn and right through the roof. Another crack rent the air, its echo tolling through the yard and into his bones. Sparks flew, igniting tree and roof in spite of the rain.

Wrapping his arms around Luci's head and using his body as a shield, he covered her. As burning bits of exploding branches fell all around them, he maneuvered her away from the fall zone.

The electric fireworks snapped, crackled and popped

and lit up the gloom of the day with unnatural brassy light. Eyes rounded and fixed on the sparking flames, she gripped his dress shirt. "The goats!"

"I'll get them." He didn't want her inside a burning building that could crash around her, so he pushed her toward the safety of the house. "Call the fire department."

Once he was sure she was heading back toward the house, he raced inside the barn, smoke already starting to thicken, and carried each frightened goat to the outdoor pen. As he lowered the bleating Fiona into the pen, Luci ran back outside, heading for the barn.

Coughing the smoke from his lungs, Dom caught up to her short of the sliding door and needed to use the advantage of his greater weight to stop her. "The goats are all safe."

"Let me go! I have a growing season's worth of stuff in there," she said, fighting his hold on her.

"You can't go in there. The roof could collapse. And if that doesn't get you, then the smoke will."

"This is my living."

"It's replaceable. You're not."

"You don't understand."

He did. For six years, she'd fought to gain her balance, to prove her independence and now her proving ground was going up in smoke. Her sense of loss twisted in his chest, made him ache for her. He wrapped his arms tightly around her, love and heartbreak tearing through him. Quick, shallow puffs of her breath panted against his throat, making him wish he could swallow her sorrow. "I understand."

She wouldn't go inside the house and insisted on

watching the barn, part of her world, burn. Torrents of rain poured over them, icing raw emotions, making the scene waver like some sort of horror show.

By the time the volunteer fire crew arrived, flames, fed by dry wood and straw of the barn, had engulfed the building.

After the fire was out, only the charred skeleton of the barn remained. The roof was gone. The firemen stowed their gear on their truck, then one of them approached. "Any reason you'd use explosives to take that tree down?"

Luci stiffened in his arms. "Explosives?"

"Someone drilled a hole, stuffed it with explosives and gave that tree a hand in coming down."

"That's crazy. This is a working farm. I have—had— animals in that barn. Why would I risk hurting them? Why would I blow up a tree on a day like this?"

The fireman didn't seem convinced. "The fire inspector'll be wanting to talk to you."

"And me him!"

The felling of the tree was intentional, not something Mother Nature had intended.

Uneasiness tightened Dom's gut. The tracking device he'd planted on Swanson's car had shown no movement since last night when Swanson had returned home to his Nashua apartment, one floor above his office. The P.I. Seekers had hired for surveillance downtown said he had a visual on Swanson in his office. If Swanson wasn't responsible for this, then who was? And why?

GETTING LUCI OUT OF the rain and inside the house took more effort than he'd expected. Her gaze was glued to the blackened barn, now roofless, as if she could rebuild it with the strength of her will alone.

He sat her down in the kitchen, poured her a cup of coffee—still hot, despite the power failure—and molded her hands around it. The last thing she needed was caffeine, but the warmth would stop her shivers. Her fingers gripped the stoneware with white-knuckled ferocity while rain ran down her cheeks like tears.

He found clean towels in the linen closet and wrapped one around her shoulders. He unplaited her braid and proceeded to dry her hair with a second towel, wishing he could make the world right for her. Hadn't she suffered enough already? Hadn't Cole's death shattered her world enough? Swanson would pay for the grief he'd added to her already overloaded burden. "It's okay to cry."

"I don't want to cry." She bit the words out as if they were tough leather. "I want to scream."

A roar exploded out of her, launching her to her feet and unseating the towel draped around her shoulders.

"I want to break something." She flung her coffee cup against the refrigerator, where it shattered and dripped dark brown rivulets against the pristine white door. Maggie cowered in her bed, eyeing them both with worry. Luci paced the kitchen floor like a wild animal, the strands of her wet hair a crazed cat-o'-nine-tails. "I want to punch something. I've put my whole life into creating this safe place for Brendan, then that jerk—"

He put himself in the path of her fist aimed at a wall, cushioning its pummel. The force of her stinging blow bruised his deltoid and drove in her anguish. He caught her wrists in his hands. "I'm sorry I brought you into this. I should've found a different way to get to Swanson."

Her hands clutched his shirt painfully. Her throat worked around the buildup of heartache she was fighting to hold back. Her voice splintered as if someone was shredding her alive. "I put my *soul* into the soil. All I wanted was a second chance. Was that too much to ask?"

He cupped her face in his palms. Tears shone in her eyes, and he wanted to tear Swanson apart. "No, darlin', it wasn't too much. And you're not going to start giving up now. You're a fighter."

"It's all gone. The herbs, the packaging, the equipment. The whole damn barn…" She shook her head. "I can't start over. Not again."

"You don't have to go through this alone. I'm here for you, Luci. I've always been."

Her chest heaved and she shook her head. Her despair tore at him. He dragged her closer, breathing his invitation into her ear. "You're a fighter. We'll nail Swanson. We'll rebuild your barn. I love you. I always have. I can help you make the life you want for Brendan."

HE LOVED HER?

Pulling back, hands knotted into the wet cotton of his shirt, Luci stared into Dom's eyes. Blue, so pale, like a soft spring sky, clear, pure. True. He loved her. He was there for her. For an instant, those words stabilized the rough currents blustering through her.

He'd been there for her from the first day she'd met

him. He'd negotiated a peace between her and Cole and the rest of the men on the team that led to acceptance. He'd boosted her confidence through the hell of training. He'd stood at her side at Cole's funeral. He'd coached her through Brendan's birth.

And he was there for her now. Dom, always Dom. Why had she not seen this before?

She could lose herself in him and still find her way out. The shock of the realization stirred up the deluge inside her waiting to burst. Like wind in a tunnel, anger, pain and guilt whipped inside her and twisted into a funnel.

"Why?" Always why. That question was a cry from her soul, ripping out of her like a volcano that had stood dormant for too long. "Why did Cole have to die? Why does Brendan have to grow up without a father? Why did you have to show up now when my life was just beginning to settle down? Why does Warren have to hurt Jill? Why did the barn have to burn with half my life inside it?"

And why was she turning to Dom yet again to find her footing?

"Because, because, because." The calming rhythm of Dom's voice, the steadiness of his hands on her back, the solid mass of his body allowed her to find her way through her inner storm.

He knew her inside out. He took her as she was and never asked her to change. He encouraged her to be true to herself.

He was there for her.

Always.

Now that the tempest had been unleashed, she couldn't seem to stop the coming tornado.

Tears climbed up her throat, vibrated their pain against his neck. Her fists struck at his shoulders even as her mouth sought solace from his. He took it all in, her torment, her sorrow, her rage.

And then she wanted more. She was tired of cold and death and destruction. She wanted heat and life and restoration.

Her hands stopped beating at the hard flesh of torso, sought warm skin beneath the wet cold of his shirt. She liked the feel of his skin under her palms, hard and smooth. She liked the clean smell of him, like summer rain. She liked the taste of him, blistering with heat. She needed the reassuring beat of life drumming in him to pound in her.

"Luci," he said, breathless, his turbulent pulse pushing her deeper into her inner maelstrom.

"I want to feel again, Dom." The kiss she pressed on him was brutal. "Let me feel."

She backed him toward the guest room, teeth nipping at his earlobe, down his neck into that wonderfully tender hollow of his throat. His heart kicked against hers, spurring her on.

She clawed at his shirt, at his pants, shed her own wet clothes. They tumbled onto the futon. He tried to slow her down as she pressed him flat against the navy blue comforter and rose above him, but his efforts only stoked her need to reach the calming eye of the hurricane that was in him.

She drank in his heat. With greedy hands, she feasted on the hard planes of his body, shoulders, pecs, flat stomach, lower. His groan came like the thunder, stirring hot bolts of anticipation. Regrets could come later.

She had no room for them now when she was once
more fighting for her survival.

She joined herself to him, threw back her head at the
rightness of the fit, rode him until her system roared
with the impending detonation of release. Then a hint
of fear kicked in. But he didn't let her fall. As always,
he caught her, holding her hips cradled in his big hands.
Safe. Each stroke, each touch, each kiss a reminder she
could surf the wild sea and make it home. The wave of
pleasure heightened until the tension, the fury, the soul-
deep anger ripping through her, crested, crashed and
broke, leaving her drained, limp and dazed, the horror
of the morning nothing more than mist.

He loved her.

"Luci." Fingers gripped into the tangle of her hair, he
rolled her under him. The tenderness softening his features, the deep longing so open in the blue of his eyes
mesmerized and she could not pull her gaze away.
Above her, his pupils widened like the lens of a camera,
giving her a glimpse into his soul, taking her breath
away.

The eye of the hurricane. Peace.

In that instant, she wanted to give him the world,
wanted him to take what he needed, wanted to erase the
edge of sorrow that flitted into his eyes. Framing his
face in her hands, she kissed him deeply, let down the
barriers she kept against the world, offered herself to
him in a way she never had to anyone before.

"Luci." The waft of his harsh whisper in her mouth
echoed inside her. And when he emptied himself in her,
her body thrummed with purpose reborn.

REGRET DIDN'T TAKE long to gallop in. By the time Luci had crawled out of his bed and climbed into a blistering shower, she couldn't help wondering if she and Dom could truly put the past behind them. Could they leave Cole behind when seeing him in Brendan brought him alive every day? Was a relationship with Dom a betrayal of Cole?

Making love to Dom seemed to have heightened his protective instincts toward her. Convincing him to continue his investigation of Warren and leave her alone in her own home had sapped away most of Luci's energy. He'd refused to leave until he'd documented both the barn and the tree, taken samples to send to Seekers and done a thorough check of the house. She'd pointed out that with two Seeker sentinels watching the house, no one was likely to come after her and his time would be better spent getting something on Warren than babysitting her. He hadn't denied he was having her watched. And after what had happened to the barn, she couldn't say she was sorry he was.

She sat cross-legged on the swivel chair, cup of coffee in hand, staring at the computer while MapQuest churned the third address Warren had given her mother through its brain. The power had been off until half an hour ago, which left her with half an hour before she had to go pick Brendan up at school.

Dom was a friend. He couldn't be a lover. Did he really love her? Or was he just feeling sorry for her? Things between them should stay behind their clearly defined lines. But lately everything was blurring—as if the world were seeking to readjust itself. And the odd longing to see that look on Dom's face again, the depth of soul, the peace so healing in them, flared much too strongly for comfort. She'd almost asked him to stay, to hold her for just a while longer.

She stared into the dark liquid in her cup. Maybe Dom was right. Maybe it was time to give up the crutch of caffeine to get through the day. The way her nerves constantly jangled couldn't be healthy.

The computer screen changed and told her there was no such address.

Andrew and Alyssa Jones and John Stone had proven common names that rendered her plenty of hits, but revealed no information. Even the specific addresses had gotten her nowhere. Warren's friends must be merpeople or dolphins because both addresses had landed her in the middle of water: Tampa Bay and the Indian River. And Christopher Bell must be a fish because, according to this map, his address would have put him square in Lake Okeechobee.

Luci reached for the Rand McNally atlas in the magazine rack beside the sofa and turned to the Florida map.

Even in the randomness of Warren's choices, a pattern emerged. All of those fictional addresses created a belt across central Florida. Because he was familiar with the area and, when pressured by her mother, he'd reverted to the familiar? And how would narrowing Warren's territory help her? Searching that area was still like looking for that proverbial needle in a haystack.

Luci decided to let the questions mull and picked up the list of phone numbers for Warren's previous victims. She plugged in Carissa Esslinger's name, hoping to find a current address and phone number.

What popped up did nothing to calm her jittering nerves. Carissa Esslinger's obituary. She'd died six months ago in a car accident. The same way she'd met Warren. Coincidence always rang bells of alarm. The obituary was stingy with details and Luci desperately needed more information. Seeing that her sister Clara Pressler survived Carissa, Luci did a search on the sister and came up with a telephone number.

"Hello?" came the harried voice on the other end of the line. A kid's movie and what sounded like a couple of toddlers filled the background with a cacophony of noises.

"Is this Clara Pressler?" Luci asked, fishing around the top of her desk for a fresh pad of paper.

"Yes."

"My name is Luci Taylor. My sister is currently engaged to the same man who conned your sister, Carissa, out of her investments. I'd really like to ask you a couple of questions if I could."

A gasp. Then silence thick and heavy pulsed across the country. "Please, Ms. Pressler. Wayne ruined your sister's life. I'd really like to put him in jail before he ruins my sister's. She has a seven-year-old son who needs her."

"I—I don't know what I could say to help you."

"Please, I need for you to answer a few questions."

Hesitation again. A peal of laughter from the kids. Was Clara watching her children, thinking about Carissa's boy, now motherless? When she answered, her voice was full of tears. "I'll try."

"Thank you. I really appreciate your help. When I was trying to find phone numbers to talk to some of Wayne's victims—"

"Victims?"

"Four, at least. My sister is his fifth. I came across an obituary for your sister. I am truly sorry for your loss. I have a bad feeling and would really like to know how she died."

"He killed her." Once Clara got started, she built up steam and couldn't seem to stop. "That son of a bitch killed her. They said it was an accident. But Carissa didn't drink. She never did. *Never*. Not before Wayne. Not after Wayne. As bad as he hurt her, she didn't drink. And why would she wait two years after he left? The cops, they wouldn't listen to me. They said I was just grieving, that I had to look facts in the face. They said she got drunk because of what Wayne did to her. That she got into her car and drove straight into a telephone pole in the middle of the night. Suicide, they said. But they didn't know Carissa. She would never do something like that, not to Nicky. She'd never leave her son that way." Clara's words strung on a tremor. "She loved him too much."

"I believe you. He did the same thing to another woman after Carissa. I want to stop him before he does it again. What can you tell me about Carissa and Wayne's relationship?"

By the time Luci hung up, she was late picking up Brendan and had a picture of Warren that was truly terrifying.

Chapter Ten

The rain gave Luci an excuse to allow Brendan to plunk down in front of the television. He'd wanted to explore the burned-out barn. That reminded her she needed to arrange for cleanup before Brendan got hurt playing in the mess. Between the loss of a season's worth of dried herbs, her store of packaging and her equipment, not to mention the chickens and the water pump, Luci's checkbook was taking quite a beating. After setting enough aside for Brendan's education, she'd spent what she'd inherited from her grandfather on buying and building this farm. And making it on her own was a point of pride.

Maybe it was time for a change. Brendan was in school now. She could take a part-time job. *Doing what, Luci?* Flipping burgers? It wasn't as if snipers were in hot demand, especially if they hadn't fired a weapon in seven years and could probably no longer hit the broad side of a barn.

She shook her head and rolled the chair closer to her work desk in the living room. This is what she wanted. A quiet life. The ties of a community—as dysfunctional as Marston could sometimes be. A safe environment for

Brendan. She waved away the dueling images of the burned barn and the balm of Dom's eyes. Did he really want a life with her and Brendan, or was it simply a misguided sense of responsibility toward his best friend's wife and son?

She looked over at Brendan, who was sprawled over his usual nest of pillows on the floor, an arm slung over Maggie. The mutt carefully watched every kernel of popcorn that went from bowl to mouth, scooping up the overflow from Brendan's tiny fist. He was a happy boy. Even growing up without a father, he was still a well-adjusted child.

Then the memory of Dom reading to him invaded her mind, filling her with an odd kind of melancholy. She looked away from her son and turned back to the computer; the sigh she couldn't contain heaved out. This quiet life couldn't be Dom's dream.

But if they stopped Warren, saving Jill's future, if not her happiness, was still possible.

The DVD of *Wishbone* episodes would keep Brendan happy for a bit before restlessness drove him to other mischief. The noise of the television and the distance of the desk would keep Brendan oblivious to her conversation.

She picked up the phone and dialed. Still no answer at Sharlene Vardeman's home. Luci didn't leave another message. She didn't want the woman to think a nut was stalking her. Katheryn Chamber's number also yielded an offer to leave a voice mail message. Luci declined. She'd verified both numbers. All she could do was keep trying until she got a hit.

After rereading the interviews of Laynie's friends,

Luci looked up their numbers and reached Marilu Bartles. The bond of someone having scammed a loved one quickly overcame their being strangers. Marilu was more than willing to dish the dirt on Willis Morehouse.

Luci had written down the questions she wanted to ask and started going down the list. "How did he meet Laynie?"

"Her parents love to entertain and they give great parties. He was the date of Laynie's friend, Gwyn Witmer."

"How good of a friend was Gwyn? Was she someone Laynie would have trusted?"

"She met Gwyn at a day spa in Dallas."

"Gwyn's from Dallas?"

"No, Austin. They were both in Dallas at the same time."

Another coincidence. A planned one?

"They hit it off right away," Marilu said. "And Gwyn liked to go to museums, so when Laynie wanted to go see an exhibit, she'd call Gwyn. I wasn't a big one for looking at pictures of slashes of paint and oohing and aahing at the artist's genius when my kid could do the same. I like to recognize what I put on my wall, you know."

"I can understand that. Do you have a phone number for Gwyn?"

"Not a current one. She moved a few months ago to be closer to her sick mother."

"Moved to where?"

"I don't remember. She wasn't my friend."

Checking with the post office probably wouldn't yield anything, but you never knew. Gwyn had moved less than a year ago, so they could get lucky. Luci made a note on the pad of paper. "Did Willis give Laynie anything?"

"Like what?"

Thinking of Jill's ring that Dom had said belonged to Laynie, Luci said, "Jewelry."

A long whoosh of air traveled through the connection. "Well, there was the ring, of course. And a pendant. A round diamond on a gold chain. She said he said it reminded him of her smile." Marilu made a gagging sound.

"That's what he told my sister, too." Luci shook her head. Warren didn't even bother with new lines. He just recycled the old ones. "Did Laynie still have the pendant after he left?"

"I don't know. I don't remember seeing it on her. But that doesn't mean anything. She was so distraught, I didn't notice anything but her tears."

"That makes sense," Luci said. Poor woman. Jill was going to be just as devastated when she learned the truth about Warren. If she had any say, Jill wouldn't share Laynie's heartbreak. "Can you tell me what the ring looked like?"

"A big emerald surrounded by diamonds. He said it was sentimental. That it belonged to his mother."

A wash of nausea burned Luci's throat. The description matched the ring that Warren had given Jill. Had Warren taken the ring off a dead woman's finger to give to his next victim? "What did he say about his family?"

"That he didn't have any. Parents dead. No siblings."

Same old, same old. "Tell me about the wedding."

Marilu sighed. "Well, the whole thing was trouble right from the start."

"Why was that?"

"Laynie's mama, she wanted a big party, you see. Her little girl was getting married. Even if it was for the third time. Willis would have none of it. He didn't want a big fuss, he said. He wanted to get on with their life together, him, Laynie and Clinton—that's Laynie's boy."

"So who won?" Luci asked, guessing it wasn't Laynie's mother. Just as her own mother was finding Warren an adept adversary at thwarting her plans.

"Surprisingly, Willis did," Marilu said, and Luci would practically see the pout across the miles. "The ceremony was short and sweet. Not that I know this personally, mind you. I wasn't invited." Hurt trudged through Marilu's voice. "He wouldn't even let her have any of her old friends as attendants. Too fussy, he said. So it was just Laynie's parents. Clinton was ring bearer. And the preacher. They all went to the Galveston beach house and had the ceremony at sunset on the beach."

Symbolic? An end to Laynie's life as she knew it? Could one person be so devious? "Where did they go on their honeymoon?"

"On a three-day cruise to the Bahamas."

Luci's heart jumped in her chest. Her voice came out as a squeak. "From Florida?"

"They flew to Miami and boarded a ship there."

Luci gasped. Miami, where Jill had been last March— right before Laynie had died.

AT FIVE THIRTY-SIX, Dom arrived to a house in chaos and Luci oblivious to it all. Did she want to avoid thinking about the mind-blowing sex they'd shared earlier? God, he loved her. He wanted to walk over to her, take her in his arms and kiss her senseless. But after her shower, she hadn't been able to look directly at him, regret clear in all of her actions. He looked away, regrets of his own seeping a weary weight through his limbs.

Brendan had quite a complicated setup of Matchbox cars, orange plastic track, cans, cookies and sandwiches spread out over the kitchen table. Maggie sat on a kitchen chair, licking peanut butter and jelly that had missed its bread target. Luci was bent over the desk in the living room, her hand racing across a pad of paper.

Dom shooed the dog off the chair. "What's up, sport?"

"Mom's talking on the phone."

"I can see that. How long has she been like that?" Was she on to a promising lead?

"Forever!" Brendan stood on a chair, launched a car down a piece of raised track. The car flew down the track, rode air over the obstacle course of oatmeal cookies and landed with a splat into an open-faced pond of peanut butter-and-jelly-laden bread. Brendan shouted his delight. Maggie sniffed at a spatter of strawberry jelly on the linoleum, then licked it.

"Did you see the barn?" Brendan asked, his eyes bright with little boy wonder.

"I sure did."

"It all burned down." He perched two cars, one behind the other, then let go. One jammed against a cookie. The other landed upside down in the peanut butter sandwich. "Mom won't let me go see."

"It's dangerous. The walls could fall on you."

Brendan's bottom lip jutted out. "That's what she said, too."

The normalcy of the chaos around him, despite the dire circumstances, set off a yearning he shouldn't dwell on. As much as he loved Luci, her heart wasn't his. And she'd made it clear enough there was no room in her world for him. After Swanson was in jail, she would close the book on their relationship.

He'd spent a frustrating afternoon keeping Swanson under surveillance. As if he knew he was being watched, Swanson had done nothing, except sit at his desk and work on his computer. Dom would've given anything to take a peek at the screen, but all he could do was watch from the outside and wait while he followed up on leads that turned into a series of dead ends. All the while he couldn't help worrying about Luci—even if she could take care of herself and had two Seekers watching her back.

An unproductive day like the one he'd had made him ravenous and the thought of one of Luci's home-cooked dinners had given him a touch of lead foot while driving home. Home? He shook his head and looked around the wreck of a kitchen. When had that shift happened? A slump of disappointment sank through him at the thought of a cold peanut butter-and-jelly sandwich for dinner.

"You hungry?" Dom asked Brendan.

"Nah." With admirable care and precision, Brendan launched another car. It ran right off the table and crashed in Maggie's water bowl, splashing water all over the floor. His hoot of delight should have caught Luci's attention. "Did you see that?"

"I sure did. That's quite a splash." Dom wasn't as good a cook as Luci, but he could throw something to-gether. Luci probably hadn't eaten anything nourishing all day. The coffeepot was full, though. What number was she on? Three? Four? "Hey, do me a favor, sport?"

"What?" Brendan stuffed cars in his jeans pocket, readying for a multiple launch.

"We're going to have dinner soon. Tell me which you'd rather do. Put the cars away or wipe up the peanut butter and jelly?"

"Aww." Brendan's face fell, fully aware playtime was over. "Put the cars away." How such a small body could put so much sulk into the words amazed him. Cole was like that, too. Always one for fun and games, but never one for cleanup.

"Why don't I get some water in the sink and you can take your cars through a car wash?" Dom said, capping the peanut butter jar. "They'll go faster next time if they're clean."

"Really?" Brendan checked the underside of one of his peanut butter-gummed racers.

"Guaranteed."

Dom ran water into the sink, added some dish detergent and settled Brendan to the task of washing up, knowing full well he was creating more of a mess than already existed.

A check with the surveillance team told him Luci hadn't moved from her spot in the living room for several hours, that they were getting a kick out of the kid's imagination and that the only human to cross the property line all day was the rural mail delivery postman.

Luci hung up the phone and signaled him to come over.

"You got something?" he asked, chomping on an oatmeal cookie.

She nodded, her hand resuming its race across the paper. "First, do me a favor. Freezer. Second shelf on the left."

"What?"

"There's a shepherd's pie there for days like this. Stuff it in the oven at three-seventy-five and we'll have dinner in an hour."

He did as she asked and slid the casserole into the oven, checking on the temperature setting and Brendan's progress before he returned to the living room. She twirled the chair around. Her green eyes were on fire. His body's reaction was instant and painful.

"I know how Warren found Jill," Luci said, her voice barely above a whisper to keep Brendan from overhearing. She pulled a sheet from beneath the pad of paper and thrust it at him. "Look at the photo. It's from March of this year, when Jill was visiting her friend Andrea in Miami."

The newspaper article was from a charity event, featuring kids and dogs. Andrea, Andrea's husband and Jill were in the foreground. Jill's smile had a flustered edge. Children were running around in the background, but a dejected Jeff hung on to his mother's hand as if he'd lose her if she let go. Jill's fingers were clasped around Jeff's hand just as tightly. Neither was feeling too comfortable.

Luci pointed at the date. "It was taken the same week Warren—or should I say Willis?—was in Miami to take his new bride on a three-day honeymoon cruise."

Dom whistled. "That's ballsy. Picking out your next pigeon before you're even done with the current one."

"That's what I thought."

"It's circumstantial, though. He could argue it was just coincidence and that he never saw the paper."

"But it's one more link of the chain."

She took back the newspaper article and placed it under the pad of paper. "I talked to a couple of people today. Jill's ring?"

"What about it?" Dom loosened the tie and pulled off the choking noose. Why couldn't Swanson take on a jeans-and-T-shirt kind of role?

"It wasn't Laynie's ring," Luci said. "Warren also gave Carissa Esslinger, victim number three, a similar one. If it's not the same ring, then it's a dead ringer. What if he gives the ring to *all* his victims?" Prickles of excitement punctuated Luci's voice. Seeing her shimmer with life like that brought back the Luci he'd fallen in love with all those years ago.

"And Jill's necklace?" Luci continued, energy bouncing off of her like solar flares. "The one that reminds him of her smile? He gave a similar one to Laynie and Carissa." Luci scoffed and shook her head, bouncing her braid over her shoulder. "Along with the same tired line. He's got his act down to an art."

"Yeah, that he does."

Luci tapped the end of her pen against her notes. "I'll need to confirm with the other two victims, but if the pattern holds, doesn't that go toward intent?"

"It sure will."

The satisfaction beaming on her face attracted him like the sun. She was so damned sexy with her blond hair all messy and her green eyes so vibrant. He wanted to kiss her, wrap himself around her, make love to her again until they were both breathless. He wanted to do it slowly until, when she looked at him, she saw *him* and the picture pleased her. But to her, he was nothing more than Cole's friend, part of her nightmare. Cole was every woman's dream of a lover with his bad-boy looks and his high-voltage energy.

He wasn't Cole, but he wasn't a consolation prize, either. He'd get the job done, nail Swanson, then he'd court Luci like he should've done twelve years ago. He could give Luci the stability she'd wanted and never had with Cole. He grabbed a sponge off the counter and started in on the peanut butter and jelly smeared table.

"It feels good, you know." The hint of longing in Luci's voice made him look up from his task. She leaned against the archway between the kitchen and living room. "To be doing something."

Never letting go of Luci's gaze, he handed pieces of plastic track to Brendan to wash. He lowered his voice, so only she'd hear his words. "Why are you hiding here?"

Her arms crossed under her chest. "I'm not hiding. This is the life I want. The life I've chosen."

"You can't hide what you are, no matter how hard you try. Maybe that's why you're having a hard time fitting in with the soccer-mom crowd."

"What's that supposed to mean?" Her body went ice-stiff.

Definitely a sore spot with the lady. "You're a fierce, intelligent woman, Luci. You were meant to lead, not cow your spirit to some artificial code."

"I can never hold a weapon again."

Interesting the leap she'd made. He hadn't suggested she go back to a sniper's life. "You're not holding a weapon now, but your true colors are showing. Did you hear yourself? It feels good to be doing something. Those are your own words, Luci."

Her chin cranked up. "This is the way I always am."

"Really?" He cocked his head and narrowed his gaze. "That's not what I saw at the soccer field. Stop trying to bend yourself into a shape you're not."

"You have no right to—"

"All done!" Brendan yelled, cutting off Luci's harsh whisper. He lifted his arms above his head, dripping water all over himself, the chair and the floor.

"That's great, sport. Why don't you climb down and put those cans where you took them?" Dom handed Brendan the first two cans he'd used to elevate part of the track, his gaze holding Luci's face like a target. As Brendan went across the room to the pantry, Dom leaned toward Luci and said in a low voice, "You tie me up in knots, Luce. You always have. I stayed away because you asked me to. I can see now I didn't do you any favor."

"Dom, don't—"

"Hear me out, Luce. There's something right between us, something good. After this case is over, I'm not leaving. I'm going to shake you up. I'm going to turn you inside out. We're going to talk about Cole. And we're going to settle things once and for all. Then, and only then—if you still want me to—will I walk away."

She opened her mouth to speak, but he cut her off. "No arguments, darlin', not unless you want to start now." He brushed up close to her, gave her the full bore of his intentions. Her eyes flared wide. Her throat worked hard. And the pulse at her neck gave a jump that revved his blood. But she didn't run away and that, more than anything, gave him hope. Why had he waited so long? He deepened his drawl to a low rumble. "Next time we make love, it won't be to fight off a demon."

DOM'S PROMISE had echoed through every cell of her body and kept her awake more efficiently than a pot of double-strength coffee could have. She'd tossed and turned all night to the memory of the soft thunder of his voice. The seed of the image he'd planted in her brain budded and bloomed until she wished he'd put an end to the torture by walking through her bedroom door and into her bed.

Crazy. Really crazy. This was Dom. Cole's best friend. The guy she'd cursed by every name in the book while she'd pushed Brendan out of her body. Was there any more undignified moment in a woman's life than that? In spite of her earlier lapse in judgment, she couldn't want him that way. That was crazy. Wasn't it?

But he'd said he loved her.

At least she hadn't had to deal with him this morning. He'd left while she was out milking the goat. Even then, even across the yard, he'd packed his grin with the promise of return that thrilled inside her. *Shut up, Luci.* There wouldn't be a next time. There couldn't be.

In the living room, Luci stared at the piece of paper in front of her.

1. Sell the goats.

As much as it pained her, she'd have to sell her does. The weather was turning too cool for them to be in the outdoor pen, and there was no way she could rebuild a shelter for them fast enough. Their milk production had already halved. Which was just as well, since she had nowhere to store the milk.

2. *Try Sharlene Vardeman and Katheryn Chamber again.*

Odds were she'd catch them at home sooner or later.

Before Luci could get to three, Jill's Lexus pulled into the driveway. Luci scrambled to hide the evidence of her search before Jill unlocked the door with her key and stepped into the kitchen. She didn't think Jill could handle the truth until it was irrefutable.

"What happened to your barn?" Jill asked, plunking her purse on the table.

"It burned down." Luci stuffed the last of her notes into a folder.

"How?" The scrape of a cup and the pouring of coffee traveled across the room.

Luci jammed the file into the desk's tiny drawer. "A tree fell on the electric wire."

Jill stepped inside the living room and winced. "How are the goats taking it?"

Luci swiveled the chair and let out a sad sigh. "I'm going to have to find them a new home."

"That's too bad." Jill cocked her head. "Are you okay?"

"I'll deal with it." She always did.

"Does that mean our date's off?"

Date? What date?

"You forgot, didn't you?" Jill's face melted.

Jill had called last night when Luci was still reeling for Dom's promise to make love to her again. "No, the wedding dress. I'm all over it. I just got off the phone with the insurance company and I'm a bit rattled. Everything in triplicate, you know."

"If you're too busy…"

"No, I want to go. I don't need to be here when the adjuster does his thing. Besides, it's not every day my sister gets to buy a wedding dress. I'm really glad you asked me. We haven't had a chance to spend much time together lately." Not with Warren cooping Jill up from those who loved her in order to keep her fully under his control.

Jill's face lit up. "Mom's going to pick up the boys from school, so we don't have to worry about getting back in time. You know how unpredictable Boston traffic is."

"Let me change and I'll be ready to go."

She grabbed the phone and hurried upstairs. Dom's line was busy, so she left him a message with her plans, regret trickling through her that she'd missed the caress of his voice. Black pants, red sweater, leather clogs. That would have to do.

Jill talked nonstop all the way into Boston. She parked near an exclusive bridal shop and was received like a queen by Zelda, the ancient shop owner.

Zelda's gray hair was pulled back into a dignified twist. The soft drape of her purple dress flowed around her trim figure smoothly. Her makeup, tasteful and natural, brightened a face unafraid to show the character it had earned. Luci hoped she looked half as good as Zelda when she reached that age.

She was thankful all she had to do was sip coffee and ooh and aah at each dress Jill tried on. Knowing how the whole affair was going to end pressed a heavy weight on Luci's chest and made it hard to work up real enthusiasm. Jill was so happy and Warren was going to crush her with his betrayal. Not spilling all she'd found took all of Luci's control. Jill wouldn't believe her. Not yet.

Zelda allowed Jill to try on all the frilly and fussy dresses she wanted, then skillfully maneuvered her toward a leaner style that showed off her curves and allowed her baby sister's natural beauty to shine through. "Wow, Jill! That's the one. You look gorgeous."

Color flooded Jill's cheeks as she twirled in the three-way mirror. "I do. I feel like a princess."

Zelda's chest puffed up. "Was I right or was I right?"

"You were right, Zelda," Jill said, her hazel eyes dewy with moisture. "I love it."

"Okay, then. Let's hem you up properly. Are those the size heel you're going to wear?" Zelda helped Jill up a small platform, then set about pinning the hem of Jill's dress. "So tell me about your young man. You're doing things right, I hope. Protecting yourself. So many silly young girls come through here with stars in their eyes and not much upstairs. I can tell you're one of the smart ones. Me, I've seen enough heartache to know how the real world works. Cross the *T*'s, I say. Dot the *I*'s."

"He's a real gentleman," Jill said. Her fingers admired the flowing cowl of the cream silk. "He would never hurt me."

"That's what they all say before the wedding." Zelda's knees creaked as she shifted position. "Then after the honeymoon, everything changes. Have your lawyer draw up a prenuptial agreement. Trust old Zelda on this, honey."

Luci gripped her flimsy coffee cup with both hands, breath held, waiting for Jill's answer.

"Warren insisted on one," Jill said, pride filling her voice.

He had? That didn't sound right for a guy who planned on sucking her dry. Was Jill really different to him than all the others? She fit the pattern so well.

"Ah, you got a winner, then," Zelda said through the pins in her mouth. "Lucky girl."

"I told him it wasn't necessary. That I trusted him."

Luci swallowed her groan with a sip of coffee before it escaped. The guy was brilliant. Offer the one thing that would make his pigeon trust he wasn't after her money. Once she was satisfied he was for real, there was no need to go through the exercise.

Zelda tsked. "Take him up on it, honey. If you're right, it makes no different. The paperwork stays in the safe. If you're wrong, you're protected. A quarter turn to the right, honey."

Jill turned, her face now hidden from view. "Zelda's right, Jill. You need to protect Jeff's future, if not your own."

Jill's shoulders heaved in a series of fast hiccups.

"Now, now, honey. Zelda didn't mean to make you cry. I tell all my girls to look out for themselves." Zelda pulled a tissue from the accent table beside her and handed it to Jill.

"I'm sorry," Jill sniffed. "It's all just such a lot of fuss. I love Warren and he loves me. All we want to do is be together. Everyone else is making such a big production out of the whole thing."

"Of course they do. The wedding is not for the bride."

Jill frowned down at Zelda. Zelda winked at her. "The wedding is for the bride's mother."

Jill laughed through her tears, dabbing the tissue at her eyes. "You are so right, Zelda. My mother is driving me crazy. We just wanted family to witness our vows, then a catered dinner at home. Now there are at least two dozen guests on my mother's list and it'll be held at the country club."

"What did I tell you? Weddings are for the mothers."

Shopping had energized Jill and left Luci with all the pluck of a wet dishrag. Getting Jill to talk about Warren on the ride home wasn't hard. All Luci had to remember was to keep her doubts to herself.

So far, each aspect of Warren's courtship matched the stories Luci had gotten from Laynie's friend and Carissa's sister.

As they crossed over the New Hampshire border, Luci broached the subject of how Jill had met Warren and finally to Amber Fitzgerald—the woman who had, as Luci was beginning to suspect, so conveniently introduced prey to predator.

"I didn't realize you and Amber were such good friends," Luci said, wishing her cup of take-out coffee wasn't empty.

"We weren't. I mean, I knew her. From the gym. We took a yoga class together. Then when Dana Booth went on maternity leave, Amber took over running the fitness center."

"So Amber's been around for a while."

"Yeah," Jill answered, distracted as she changed lanes for her exit. "She joined last April. And we've gotten to be good friends."

April. Right after Jill came back from Florida. Coincidence? Running a background check on Amber might be worthwhile. Warren couldn't be working alone.

"Do you see her outside the gym?" Luci asked.

"We meet at the country club for lunch once a week. That's how I ended up running into Warren. And she introduced us. She's really down-to-earth, you know. She's been a great sounding board with Mom being so difficult to deal with about the wedding and the reception."

Which was just what Warren needed. Jill turning to a stranger instead of her own family. It made conning her that much easier.

Amber looked so plain with her mousy hair and brown eyes. An ordinary and sympathetic friend. And when this mousy woman introduced the pigeon to her dashing friend, well, then, the pigeon knew Amber wasn't competition and that because he was a friend of someone so ordinary, he had to be safe.

Such a perfect ploy.

Luci couldn't wait to get home and run a background check on Amber. If she and Dom could prove that Amber had been involved in all the other cons and had introduced each victim to Warren, they might be able to get Amber to turn evidence against him.

Preferably before the wedding.

IN THE QUIET DARKNESS of Jill's home, Warren contemplated his fate. What had gotten him here, where the road would lead him next. He was tired, he realized as he sipped Jill's expensive cognac and sank into the luxurious leather of her couch. Tired of teaching the same lesson time after time, knowing he could never reach them all.

Yesterday, he'd taken the next step. He'd put down a deposit on the sailboat of his dreams. The forty-two-footer would allow him to sail the world at his leisure and fall asleep in the soothing arms of the only woman he'd ever loved—the sea.

Then his mind filled with images of the woman who'd made his life hell.

He'd thought he'd wait until he could shove his triumph in her face to reap his earned reward, but she'd already lingered longer than he'd expected and wasn't showing any signs of fading—or remembering what she'd done to him.

He couldn't help himself, he reached for the phone and dialed the number from memory.

"Blue Skies Resort," the cheerful voice chimed.

Blue skies for the doctors who ran the place, maybe. Certainly not for the patients confined within the "resort's" walls—as gilded as they were. "Room 203."

"One moment please while I connect you."

The phone rang six times before someone answered.

"It's me," he said. "How is she?"

"The same."

"Is she awake?" Some days were more lucid than others.

"Yes."

"Is she talking?"

A creak of hesitation. "Yes."

Fortifying himself with a swallow of cognac, he asked, "Has she asked for him?"

The licking of lips. "Billy, don't torture yourself this way."

"Has she?" he insisted.

"Yes, Billy, she has."

He closed his eyes, swallowed the burn of bile etching his throat. "Has she asked for me?"

A sigh of regret. "No, Billy, she hasn't."

She'd asked about the man who'd treated her like dirt, but not about the one who'd once worshipped her like a queen.

"Thank you."

He lay the phone carefully back on its cradle. Then hurled the fine crystal of the snifter at the stone fireplace. "Bitch!"

Chapter Eleven

The dream started much as it always did, with darkness sucking her into its deep hole, with Cole, bigger than life in her scope, rushing into that Texas shack. But this time, the darkness mutated to a scene Luci didn't recognize. A river, waves roped like veins and silver like liquid mercury, flowed and oozed over its banks. A black-clad figure that reeked of evil stood among the pitchy lances of trees against a bloody sky. Outfitted in white, standing out like neon among the black grass, she lay in a forward firing position, aiming her rifle at the trace of evil, an eerie green shape planted in the crosshairs of her night-vision scope. She kept squeezing the trigger at the offender, but the bullets never reached their target. They stopped midair and dropped to the ground, useless.

Not even a scalding shower could loosen the sense of failure that clung to her when she woke up. What if...? What if...? Heart pounding, she headed to the kitchen and flipped on the coffeemaker. Not wanting her restlessness to wake Dom, she headed outside.

In the past few days, she'd found a new home for her goats, dealt with the insurance adjuster and the crew demolishing her barn and dug up every scrap of information she could find on Amber Fitzgerald.

The woman seemed to have sprung to life only a year ago. Her credit history started, as did all of Warren's, in Florida. Luci had called Carissa Esslinger's sister and Laynie McDaniels's friend again and learned that the description of the woman who'd introduced their loved ones to Warren fit Amber. She'd also finally reached the first victim, Katheryn Chamber, who'd corroborated all the details. The three photos the women had e-mailed yesterday left no mistake. Amber was Warren's front-woman. The hairstyles were different, but not the plain-mouse, trust-me demeanor.

How was Amber related to Warren? Why would she do such a thing? What was she getting out of it?

Seeing the goats' pen empty only reinforced the feeling of having failed. Luci scanned at the pitiful leftovers of her garden. She hadn't had time to set up the cold frames and they'd gone up in flames with the barn. Only the kale and a few tufts of herbs remained.

She bent down and snipped chives for breakfast omelets, weariness sighing through her bones. Did she have the courage to start all over again? She ran her fingers through the cool earth she'd enriched and worked these past six years. She'd tried to grow roots. What else could she have done? She'd promised Cole on his grave that she would protect Brendan, give him a secure life, raise him to be a good, strong man.

She turned her face to golden rays of sun and breathed crisp morning air through the tightness in her chest. No use. The claw of anxiety wouldn't leave until Warren was behind bars. Jill would hate her for destroying her happiness, but at least her sister and nephew's futures would be safe.

With only a week until the wedding, the frenetic pace of the investigation had kept her mind from getting stuck on Dom and his promise that they would make love again. Just the thought made her body soften and warm—yearn. Then disappointment became a sinking stone. She couldn't let that happen again. Wrong time. Wrong place. Wrong person.

He didn't really love her. He couldn't.

Luci stood and headed back toward the house.

The elementary school's carnival was today—Jill's first event as PTO president. Brendan had saved his pennies for weeks and had had a hard time falling asleep last night anticipating the prizes he'd win. Normally, Luci enjoyed the fun and games. But all Luci could think of today was that the carnival would serve as another chance to observe Warren. Most of the community turned out for events like these. Warren would want to show he was supporting his future wife's endeavors, and Luci hoped that Amber would also choose to attend.

"Kingsley just called," Dom announced as she came into the kitchen. "Jill's moved some of her assets."

Luci's hands froze over the sink. "She bought a wedding dress on Wednesday."

Dom whistled. "I'd like to see the wedding dress that cost fifty thousand dollars."

Chives forgotten, she whipped around to face Dom. "Five thousand, not fifty." Her heart raced. Warren would wait until after the wedding to start bleeding Jill, wouldn't he? "Where did the rest of the money go?"

"She opened a new account with the full fifty. A joint account with Warren's name on it."

Luci winced. "How could Jill fall for that?"

"Just like she's fallen for everything else. He probably gave her some sort of song and dance about his investments being tied up right now. If she'd just front him the money for the honeymoon, he'd pay her back as soon as they returned from their trip."

Luci banged a frying pan onto the stove. Just the thought of Jill's heartbreak when she realized Warren had betrayed her brought bile to Luci's throat. It wouldn't come to that. "We've almost got enough to stop Warren cold."

"We'll get him." Dom came close, too close. He hooked a loose strand of her hair behind her ear. The softness of his touch scrambled any logical thought that might have formed. The look in his eyes, both keen with purpose and soft with desire, dried her mouth and left her starving for his kiss.

"I'm going to make sure I run into Amber today." Luci broke away from his disturbing touch and strode to the refrigerator to search for eggs.

"Be careful. We don't want to spook her."

Brendan chose that moment to pound down the stairs and burst into the kitchen, followed by Maggie, hyped up on Brendan's energy. "The carnival's here! The carnival's here!"

He dumped the coffee can that served as his bank on the table, spilling coins all over the surface. "Is it time to go yet?"

"Soon. Come on, scoop up those pennies and let's eat some breakfast."

THE CARNIVAL, set up on the elementary school's front lawn, was already a madhouse by the time they arrived. Luci scanned the crowd, searching for Amber and Warren. The garage sale corner on the west side was a hive of activity. Was Amber there, looking for an unexpected treasure or a future mark? Bigger kids tried their luck at the games of chance manned by teachers on the east side. Did Amber enjoy playing the odds, or was there another reason she was willing to play Warren's games? Smaller kids buzzed around the toddler area near the playground. The principal barked a spiel at the cakewalk circle by the front door. Older ladies flocked to him, but no one resembling Amber. Luci zeroed in on the people going into the cafeteria to check out the silent auction.

A discordant hum of voices, punctuated now and then with shouts, riddled the air. A myriad of high-end perfumes clashed with the scents of sugar and popcorn. But no Amber. And no Warren. Had Luci been wrong? Would they both keep away, turning this into a wasted day?

Luci caught a glimpse of Jill, looking official with her clipboard, and waved. Jill promptly signed up Luci to serve a morning shift at the garage sale tables, then an afternoon shift in the food booth to cover for no-shows. Warren, Jill told her, was running the silent auction.

Between shifts, Luci checked out the cafeteria in the guise of putting down a few bids. Out of the corner of her eye, she caught Amber talking with Warren. A taut look fractured Amber's doll-smooth face. Her fists were tight at her side. Warren's gaze darted around the room, as if to judge who was witnessing the exchange. Luci wound her way closer, using the boards describing each item to cloak her progress. But by the time she was close enough to listen in on their conversation, Amber was heading back outside and Warren had disappeared backstage. Luci followed Warren until he entered the boys' room. With a reluctant sigh, she returned outside.

As Luci served cookies, popcorn and soft drinks at the food booth, she kept searching the crowd for Amber, hoping her prey hadn't left already, willing the clock to advance so she could leave her post and actively search for Amber.

Dom, who was hanging out with the boys, hovered in the background, his gaze a constant itch between her shoulder blades. And every time she glanced in his direction and their gazes linked, her brain fried her thoughts, as if she'd accidentally stuck her finger in a socket. *Next time we make love, it won't be to fight off a demon.* Next time.

Still collecting herself after one of those searing moments, Luci spied Amber shopping the brownie table. She was small, Luci noted, almost childlike in build. Her jeans and sweater allowed her to fit in the crowd unnoticed. Neither her brown hair nor her mud-brown eyes made her stand out. How could someone like her have caused so much damage? And why?

Luci walked over to the end of the booth and offered the woman her hand over the counter. "Hi, Amber. I'm Luci Taylor. Jill's sister."

Amber shuffled a brownie from one hand to the other and gave Luci's hand a limp shake. A shy smile flickered on her lips before disappearing. "Of course. Jill talks about you all the time."

Luci would love to have overheard those conversations. "I know it's kind of last minute, but I'd really like to throw Jill a small wedding shower. I was wondering if you'd help me plan it. Surprise her after one of her yoga classes?"

Amber looked genuinely pleased at being asked. "Oh, that's so sweet of you. Of course. I'd love that. Why don't you come by the studio Monday afternoon? We could surprise Jill after her Thursday class." Amber pointed at a can of Coke at the back of the booth behind Luci. "Could I have one, please?"

Luci deliberately picked up a can of Sprite from the carton by its top and handed it to Amber. Amber grabbed the can, frowned, then handed it back. "Um, I meant the other one. The Coke."

"Oh, sorry." Luci put the Sprite can aside and handed Amber the Coke. "I'm just so excited to pull off a surprise on Jill."

"I won't breathe a word to her. I promise." Amber fished for her wallet in her purse. "How much for the brownie and soda?"

"A dollar fifty." Luci craned her neck, hoping to see something, anything, in the woman's belongings that would give her away.

Amber handed her the change, then waved. "I'll see you tomorrow. Bring ideas!"

I wouldn't miss it for the world.

After Amber disappeared into the crowd, Luci placed the Sprite can in a new paper popcorn bag and carefully put it in her purse. If Dom could get fingerprints off the can, then they could get another lead on her.

When her shift was over, Luci found Dom and Brendan at the football toss game.

"I have a date with Amber on Monday afternoon," Luci whispered, wondering again at the surge of energy rushing through her bloodstream.

"That's great." Dom's blue eyes held a secretive gleam at her barely contained excitement that made her look away. She wasn't hiding in Marston. She was trying to create a new life. Going back was out of the question. Not that the team would have her again.

"Dom, watch me!" Brendan shouted and hefted the football back.

"We need to come up with a game plan," Dom said, keeping his gaze on Brendan's mighty throw.

"Tonight," she promised. "How fast can you get fingerprints analyzed?"

One of his eyebrows rose, and she couldn't help smiling. "I have a fresh can of soda Amber touched."

"I'll see if Falconer can call in a favor."

"Falconer?"

"My boss. We should know something by tomorrow."

After his successful toss, Brendan ran not to her, but to Dom. "Did you see my pass? Did you?"

Dom clasped Brendan's shoulder with one of those manly gestures of appreciation. "I sure did. That's quite an arm you've got. You drilled it right into the target."

Brendan lapped up the praise like melting ice cream. "Auntie Jill invited us all for pizza after the carnival. You're coming, right?"

The hundred-watt smile on her son's face brought tears to her eyes and her failure sank through her like lead. She'd done this to him, made him so desperate that he'd latch on to the first man to show up on their doorstep. How could she possibly even think about returning to the life that had caused the situation?

"Of course, we're coming," Luci said with a quick glance at Dom. At least that gave them another opportunity to interact with Warren.

"Wait for me." Brendan tugged downward on Dom's hand as if to anchor him on the spot. "I gotta tell Jeff I'm riding with you."

Brendan took off toward his cousin at a run. "Jeff! Jeff!"

"I won't go if it's too hard for you." The melancholy riding the low tide of his voice, the way his gaze cut from her to Brendan had her heart tripping over itself. Did he see Cole in Brendan as she did? Did he, what? Want a relationship with her son to bring him closer to his missing friend? No, that was crazy.

But if she said she didn't want him there, then Brendan would be disappointed and she'd be the bad guy. Deciding what was best for Brendan tore her in half.

She flicked her braid over her shoulder. If Dom wanted to be a father, he'd have had kids of his own by now. Even if Brendan needed a male to look up to, she didn't need a man to share her life. A relationship with Dom would never work. Not with Cole's death a constant cross between them. She switched her purse from one shoulder to the other, holding back the sudden urge to hit something to discharge the storm building in the pit of her stomach. Then she remembered where that had landed her last time and heat raced up her neck.

"I'm fine," she said. "You need face time with Warren." She cupped a hand to her mouth. "Brendan! Let's go!"

Dom had threatened to force her to talk about Cole. But talking wouldn't change a thing. They couldn't rewrite the past. And with them, the past would always taint the future.

Out of the corner of her eye, Luci spied Sally Kennison approaching, her face set with purpose. Luci groaned and tightened her purse to her side. "Here comes trouble."

Sally barely said hello to Luci before she stuck her hand out at Dom. "Hi, I'm Sally Kennison. And you are?"

Dom cranked on his winning grin and pumped Sally's hand. "Dominic Skyralov, an old friend of Luci's."

"An old friend." Sally practically salivated with eagerness. "How interesting. Are you here for a visit?"

"I just moved to the area."

"Really? To be with Luci?"

"Sally," Luci interrupted. "Did you want something?"

Frowning, Sally plucked a receipt from her purse and handed it to Luci. "Oh, yes. I'd like an explanation please. I went to get the certificates made for the fundraiser raffle and the account was at zero. You've put me in a difficult position here."

"That's impossible. I deposited everything after Thursday's game."

Sally's crimson mouth thinned to a straight line and both her eyebrows disappeared beneath her stiff bangs. "Um, when I asked the bank manager who had cleaned out the account, he said it was you."

"He was wrong." Luci had never stolen anything in her life. Except for a candy bar when she was eleven. She'd wanted so badly to be accepted by her new friends at school she'd pocketed a Kit Kat on a dare. But she hadn't been able to eat it. She'd gone back the next day, returned the candy and never talked to those two girls again. So much for fitting in. "It says the transfer was done electronically. The way we set up the account, we'd need two authorization codes for that, and I don't know yours."

"Well, obviously you do because the money's gone."

Dom shifted, his body suddenly in ready mode. Luci took one step forward, letting him know she could handle Sally on her own.

"This is the kids' money, Luci." Sally speared her with a disapproving look down her long nose. "I realize you've had a few hardships lately, but that's no excuse to borrow what doesn't belong to you."

"Are you accusing me of stealing?" Luci's hands bunched into fists. Her? When she'd done everything to make sure those meager funds multiplied as much as they could? Sally had some nerve.

Sally shrugged, then launched an apologetic look at Dom. "Well, if the shoe fits."

"It doesn't," he assured her.

Fighting temper, Luci stuffed Sally's receipt in her purse. Whatever happened had a solid explanation that had nothing to do with theft—at least on her part. "I'll straighten this out first thing Monday morning."

"You do that." Sally clucked her tongue before spinning on her heel and leaving.

The freshening breeze abraded Luci's cheeks. The kids' shouts pierced her ears. The dying sun's last burst burned her eyes. And she became acutely aware of the curious eyes staring her down and the prickling tongues ready to toss the juicy gossip into the wind like dandelion seeds. *Did you know Luci Taylor was a thief? I heard it myself. She stole the kids' soccer club account money.*

"You okay?" Dom asked, falling in beside Luci.

"I'll live." She always did. "How did Warren do this?"

"He's got a knack for manipulating accounts." Dom hooked an arm around her shoulder, giving her a reassuring squeeze as he led her toward Jill and the boys.

Despite his support, she wanted the ground to open up and swallow her whole. "But why bother with such a small amount?"

"To make you hurt."

"He succeeded." She stifled the wrenching knot of tears at the base of her throat and refused to hide her head in the waiting crook of Dom's shoulder. Spine straight, chin up, she walked through the crowd alongside Dom. She'd done nothing wrong. But Sally's lack of faith in her still hit a tender spot. "Half the town thinks I'm a thief."

AFTER DINNER, Warren and Dom went with the boys to explore the pinball machine and the other video games in the arcade at the back of the restaurant.

"When will your dress be ready?" Luci asked, swirling the straw in her glass of iced tea. The ice chunks clinked like a series of rifles cocking.

A dreamy look spread over Jill's face. "I'm picking it up Wednesday. Do you want to come?"

"I'd love to come with you. You'll look so beautiful, Jill."

"I can't wait for next Saturday." Jill looked toward the arcade, stars gleaming in her eyes. "It's going to be the best day of my life."

Or the worst if Luci couldn't stop Warren in time. She fiddled with the salad on her plate. "I was thinking about what Zelda said about the prenuptial. I think if Dom and I get to that stage, I'll definitely take Zelda's advice. For Brendan's sake."

Jill jammed her elbows on the table and leaned forward, nose wrinkling with curiosity. "So it's serious then, between you and Dom?"

Luci shrugged. "Too early to tell. But—"

"I knew it! There's something there." Jill pointed a finger at her. "I noticed it right away, the day you brought him to the cookout. I think today the whole town noticed the way he looks at you." Jill smacked her lips. "And the way you look at him."

"You think?" Luci shuddered at the gossip that could spread.

"Positive."

"About the prenuptial—"

Jill leaned back, crossing her arms. "I trust Warren."

"I know you do. But there's Jeff."

Irritation crimped Jill's forehead. "Jeff's future is secure. J.J. made sure of that. I love Warren and he loves me. This is the real thing, Luci. We're going to grow old together."

Luci sighed. There was no winning this. Jill wasn't

going to realize her mistake until it was too late. Luci wished she could spread all the evidence on the table and show Jill what kind of man Warren was, show her how he wooed and hurt all those other women, how he'd left them heartbroken and broke—and two of them dead. But if she did, Warren would bolt, and she would be responsible for his next victim. All they needed was a few more days to figure out Amber's role in the scam, corner her and get her to testify against Warren. "That he's asking you for money before the wedding worries me."

Jill's chin cranked up defensively. Her gaze narrowed. "How do you know that?"

Shrugging, Luci covered her slip with a lie. "Mom mentioned something about it."

Jill blew out a breath that ruffled her bangs. "Does no one in this family mind their own business?"

Luci noticed Dom ambling over to the bar a couple of tables down and ordering a round of soda. A worried look crossed his face. Luci ignored it and focused on soothing her sister. "We love you, Jill. We all want what's best for you."

Jill's manicured nail drilled into the table. "Then accept Warren. He *is* the best. If you must know, that money is my wedding gift to him." Her face lit up with pleasure. "I'm buying him the boat of his dreams. He's going to teach me how to sail." She skewered Luci with a cutting scowl. "Just because J.J. didn't know how good he had it doesn't mean all men who fall for me are fools. Or that I can't find someone who loves me for me, not my bank account."

"I didn't mean—"

"But you're hurting me anyway, Luci." Each of Jill's words got tighter, sharper. "Warren's going to be my husband. I'm going to take care of him as well as he takes care of me. That's what married people do." Her voice rose to a high, thin blade as she plunked her napkin on her plate. "At least I didn't kill my own husband."

The bells on the pinball machine jangled. Silverware clanged out of tune. A tray of glasses crashed in the kitchen. Every face at the surrounding tables turned in her direction. Every one of them etched with a mixture of horror and morbid curiosity.

No, she wanted to shout. *It was an accident. I didn't kill him. I waited too long. Still my fault, but not my bullet. It's not the same. I didn't kill him.*

But that was a lie. Wasn't that what she'd told herself all these years? That she'd killed Cole. That his death was her personal debt? All her training had prepared her, but when it had come to proving herself, she'd failed. If she hadn't hesitated that extra fraction of a second, her first bullet wouldn't have missed Grigsby and he'd have been dead at the time he shot Cole. As it was, by the time she hit him with her second bullet, he'd killed Cole and both his hostages. Their deaths weighed on her soul, too.

She hadn't squeezed the trigger—and that was the crux of it all. If she had, three innocent people would still be alive.

Jill had not lied.

Luci's mistake had killed Cole.

Her fault. Her failure. Her cross to bear.

And as she watched all those faces watching her, shame burned. They would believe Jill. They would see

Luci as a murderer. As desperately as she'd wanted to become part of Marston, part of the community, she now realized that she never had—not even as a child—and never would. Trying to fit into small-town life was proving to be just another disappointment.

If she'd been an outcast before, the spilling of her secret would now make her a pariah.

With slow, deliberate movements, Luci scraped back her chair, rose, turned on her heel and marched out of the restaurant and into the cold night.

Chapter Twelve

Dom rounded on Jill. Luci was putting her life on the line to save her sister and she shouldn't have had to take a kick in the teeth like that from Jill. "You can be a real bitch, you know that. Luci didn't kill Cole. My mistake did."

That's why he'd stayed away for so long. He'd needed Luci's forgiveness and was afraid she wouldn't give it to him. He hadn't known that she blamed herself for Cole's death. All these years, he'd thought she'd couldn't stand the sight of him because he wasn't unable to defuse the situation, for letting it get too inflamed by the time the assault team was called in to put an end to the situation.

He rounded up a protesting Brendan from the arcade and caught up with Luci at his truck. She sat stiffly all the way home, staring blankly out the window.

She said nothing as they arrived, simply got out and headed toward what had once been her barn.

Dom settled Brendan with Maggie in the living room, then sought out Luci. Silently he stood beside her, staring at the concrete on which she'd once built all her hopes.

The chill in the air wasn't from the bite of September wind, but from the howl of loss. After everything she'd lost this week in the barn fire, now the sister she was trying to help had hacked at the final piece of root tying her to Marston.

Training was designed to make the trainee fail and to test how well he could overcome his own inadequacies. She'd gone through territory most people never probed—and had survived.

Twice.

She didn't need any more tempering.

He reached out for her, but she jerked her shoulder, refusing his support. His hand hung in midair for a moment, then he stuffed his fist in his jeans pocket.

"Luci…I meant what I said about helping you rebuild." They needed to talk about Cole, clear the air about his death and how it tortured them both. He loved her too much to let her bright inner flame go out completely. Words had always been his strong suit. Knowing when to talk, what to say to gain trust, calm tempers and end conflict.

Except when he'd most needed those skills, he'd failed Cole—and Luci.

"Talk to me," he said, coaxing her as he'd tried to win over the man who'd killed her husband. *Talk to me, Joe Bob. What's going on here? Is everybody okay?* "Jill should never have said what she did to you. She doesn't know what happened. She shouldn't judge."

Luci stepped away from him, arms wrapped around her middle as if she were holding herself together. "I missed my first shot." Her voice was so devoid of life it scored him like a dull knife. "Less than a tenth of a second window of error. And I missed it."

"Grigsby was a mover—unstable and unpredictable. You couldn't have predicted his movements." But he should have. That was his job. When the demands got outrageous, when rapport was unraveling, he should've let go.

"I want a million dollars in cash. A helicopter to fly me to Mexico." Grigsby screamed his demands, his voice seeming to sweat blood with his heightening anxiety.

"Okay, now we're talking. Getting those things here is going to take time. You've gotta give us some time, Joe Bob."

"No more talking. I get out or no one gets out. I want it now."

"And I want to help you. I'm on your side. The bank's closed right now. It takes at least twenty minutes to fly a copter out here. And about two hours to access that kind of money. Give me a chance to get you what you want."

"Just get it here or I'm going to kill the bitch. I'm going to kill the kid."

Luci's hollow voice reached through his memories. "No one asks you how you made a shot." She rubbed opposite arms against a chill that was seven years old. "All anyone ever cares about is why you missed."

Her pain wrapped around his heart, squeezed it painfully, and threw him back to that run-down shack, to his desperation to end the situation peaceably.

"Joe Bob, come on, talk to me. What did you take? How much? I'm trying to help you, but you've gotta give

*me something to work with. I've got my boss on the line.
He's looking into the helicopter. But he's going to want
something in exchange to show your good faith. You
send out the boy, you get you some wheels. That sound
good to you?"*

Dom had tried to keep Grigsby on the phone, to keep
him talking. The passage of time, he'd been taught,
often gave a hostage taker the chance to vent his anger
and frustration, a chance to feel listened to. But he'd
screwed up. He'd hadn't been able to connect with
Grigsby, hadn't been able to talk him down. Hadn't
been able to reason him into releasing the hostages.
The Special Operations Group leader had suggested
they try another negotiator, but Dom was convinced
that with a little more time he could establish the needed
rapport with Grigsby.

But Grigsby threw out the phone. He was done talking, done looking for a solution.

"Luci, Cole's death wasn't your fault. We should
have gone in sooner. By the time Grigsby threw out the
phone, he was too high on drugs, too unpredictable."

Grigsby had strapped a rifle to his ex-girlfriend so
that if she moved, she would kill herself. He'd wrapped
the kid around him like live body armor. The leader had
sent in the assault team.

Pop. Pop. Pop. The echo of Grigsby's three shots re-
sounded in Dom's brain as if they were happening now.
Faster than a thought and three people were dead. Then
Luci's shot—boom—and it was all over.

Blood and failure stained the ground.

Dom had joined the team for justice, for a cause, to
save lives. Making the cut, training and the successes

that came after all bred a certain feeling of invincibility. That illusion shattered the day Cole died.

For all these years, he'd thought Luci's forgiveness would free him. The truth was that he couldn't forgive himself.

"Cole died because I wasn't accurate enough," Luci insisted. The breeze fingered her hair the way Dom wished she'd let him.

The thick skin of guilt skewed her perception. "That's bull and you know it. You were good, Luci. Damned good. Grigsby would've killed a lot more of the team if you hadn't stopped him." He took in a deep breath and spewed out the words he'd needed to tell her for seven years. "And if you want to play the blame game, then Cole died because I couldn't talk Grigsby into giving up peaceably."

A short sob ripped out of her. "Talk wasn't going to work with him. He had nothing to lose."

"But we all did." Needing to touch her and reassure her, Dom risked another rejection and wrapped his arms around her and pulled her to his chest.

She looked up at him, her green eyes full of tears. In them, he could see the pieces of her heart and wanted desperately to glue them back together.

"Cole's dead," she choked out, acceptance a hard pill to swallow. "He's never coming back."

He kissed the top of her head. "Letting yourself die doesn't help him. Or you and Brendan."

"I loved him."

"I know. I loved him, too."

She pivoted her head until it lay on his shoulder. Her hands spread on his chest and his heart beat into her palms. Dom wanted to stop her pain, stop the destruction, stop the memories.

"Being with Cole," she said, the choke of feelings raw as if she'd turned herself inside out, "it was like plugging straight into high-voltage current. I needed that then. After trying to fit a square peg into a round hole all of my life, having the freedom to fly was exhilarating. He pushed me out of my comfort zone." She swallowed hard against his shoulder. "And you were the solid rock that kept me grounded when Cole took me too high, too fast. I needed that, too." She shook her head, the rest of the words she needed to release caught in the crush of her closing throat. "When I lost him, I lost part of myself."

She'd shut herself off and gone for safe, even if it wasn't her nature. "It's time you found it again," he whispered hoarsely.

Time they both did.

"I thought I'd found myself here." Her gaze went to the eerie glow of concrete in moonlight. "Being here, working the farm, raising Brendan, that kept me out of the black hole Cole's death took me into." She lifted her head and met his gaze. "Then you came."

"And brought it all back." Making him wish he'd never heard of Swanson and his scheme.

Confusion flitted across her eyes. "Something in me is coming back to life, Dom. And it scares me."

And suddenly, so was he because, for the first time in a long time, hope sang through him and made him dizzy. Hope that she could come to accept a future with him. Hope that he could give her what she needed to restore happiness in her life. Hope that they could put

Cole's ghost behind them. "Then we'll take it slow and easy."

He kissed her gently, tenderly, then nudged her toward the house and the soft halo of light surrounding it, holding on to her hand, knitting his fingers with hers. As they stepped into the kitchen the sounds of Brendan's laughter and Maggie's barks greeted them. "One step at a time. We'll figure it out."

FROM THE COCOON OF HIS CAR, Warren watched them through binoculars. Kissing like that when a child was nearby. Didn't they know the damage such a sight could cause a child?

She'd done that to him. Brought men home, seduced them. Did she think he was deaf? That he couldn't hear the bed banging against the wall, her moans, her lover's grunts?

This is the one, she'd always said. *Meet your new daddy.* The first one had shown up on his seventh birthday. But each man had never stayed more than a night. Why should they have when she'd given herself away so freely?

Then she'd done just as Jill had done yesterday—freely used the money she was supposed to spend on her son's welfare to make herself more attractive to another horny bull who only wanted a night of release.

She'd deserved what had happened to her.

They all did.

THE CLOUD THAT WAS WARREN still hung over Luci, but as she cleaned up the breakfast dishes on Monday morning, she could see blue skies ahead. The thought stuck her with a new dart of fear. Soft blue. Like Dom's eyes. Was she crazy for hoping that he really did love her? Or was she, like Jill, simply setting herself up for heartache when he left?

One day at a time. Dom was right. Given the circumstances, that was all they could hope for. Right now, they needed to concentrate on Warren and Amber. Then they'd see if there was something more between them than obligation to a dead friend.

"We've got her," Dom said as he came into the kitchen, his voice animated. "We've got Amber."

"The fingerprints paid off?" Luci forgot about the pancake griddle in the sink and joined Dom at the table.

He slapped down the small notebook he carried and took a chair. "Big time. Her real name is Davina Pedley. She's from Merritt Island, Florida. She was arrested when she was eighteen for pulling a bank-examiner type scam. She was working as an aide for an elderly woman who was sick and living alone and conned her out of her life's savings."

Luci sat beside him and tension knitted itself into her muscles. "How much time did she serve?"

"None."

She frowned. "How can that be?"

"Amber returned the money. The victim refused to press charges."

"That's crazy." Luci batted her braid over her shoulder. "She could have lost her life's savings. Did Amber's accomplices get caught?"

Dom scoffed. "Amber said she worked alone."

"Don't you need three people to make that kind of scam work?"

He glared at his notes. "She was working as an aide, so she answered the phone, took messages, ran errands, made meals. When Amber told Maude Rosenfeld that the bank was concerned someone was tapping into her account, Mrs. Rosenfeld trusted Amber with her account information. Amber took out the money herself, using Mrs. Rosenfeld's signed authorization, and would have gotten away with it if Mrs. Rosenfeld hadn't told her son about her close call. He called the police, who nabbed Amber. Lucky for us, she was booked."

Luci popped up from her chair, refilled her coffee cup and let the shot of caffeine fire her brain cells. "Tapping into accounts. That's what Warren does. And that motel room in Texas where Laynie McDaniels died was in a woman's name." She plunked her cup on the counter untouched, energy stirring through her blood. "That's it. Maybe Amber's the brains behind the scam. Maybe the name on the register is one of Amber's aliases. Where's your file?"

He jerked his head toward his bedroom. And for the briefest of moments, Luci wished he'd follow her there. She found the file in his briefcase beside the futon and dug it out.

"Either way," Dom said when she returned and set the briefcase on the table, "we need something big enough on one of them to make them crack. I'm going to make some phone calls. We'll need as much on Amber as we can and see where it leads."

"We're getting somewhere. I can feel it." Luci glanced at the clock on the stove and with a sigh of exasperation she went to the stairs. "Brendan, hurry up with that book bag. We're going to be late." She turned back to Dom, a list forming in her mind. "I'm going to drop Brendan off at school. I'll see if Jill will pick him up after school so I don't have to worry about my meeting with Amber running over if it's going well. That'll also keep Jill away from the fitness center." One hand tapped the archway. "We're going to get Amber. Today."

DOM MISSED LUCI as soon as she'd left. Even those few minutes without her filled him with a strange kind of emptiness. Over the years, he'd tried to convince himself he didn't love her, that if he truly had, he'd have fought for her, that he would have stuck around even after she'd sent him away. Irrational, stupid, wrong. But to go on without her, he'd needed the doubts. In those moments when he was honest with himself, he could admit he loved her and had never stopped loving her.

He couldn't let his feelings for her get him side-tracked. Not when he was the one who'd put her in danger. He had a job to finish before he could pursue any future with Luci.

Using an online reverse directory, Dom looked up Davina Pedley's old address.

"Hi," Dom said when a gruff voice answered the phone. "This is John Gibson of Holliday & Houghlin. I'm looking for Davina Pedley."

"Sorry, the Pedleys moved out about ten years ago."

"Well, Mr...."

"Turillo," the man supplied. "Robert Turillo."

"Mr. Turillo, I have a check here from a policy where Ms. Pedley was named a beneficiary and I'm trying to locate her. Would you know where she moved to?"

"No, I can't say that I do."

"How about the neighbors? Would anyone know where she's gone?"

A tick of silence. "Well, there's the Mullins and the Jacksons, I suppose. They've been there forever."

"Thanks, I'll give them a try. You have a good day now, Mr. Turillo."

Dom looked up both numbers and dialed the first. The Jacksons weren't home, so he moved on to the Mullins. "Mrs. Mullins? This is John Gibson of Holliday & Houghlin. Your neighbor, Mr. Turillo, gave me your name and said you could possibly help me locate Davina Pedley."

"What for?" came a brusque voice creaky with age.

"She's the named beneficiary in a policy we're holding and we're trying to locate her to pay off the benefits."

"Listen to me, young man, if Davina Pedley's involved, she's probably got you duped."

Maybe Luci was right. Maybe Amber was the scam's mastermind. By why would Swanson go along? Money? That was certainly a great motivator and they were raking it in. "Why do you say that?"

"Ha! She's done it before and if Billy hadn't sweet-talked Maude Rosenfeld into dropping the charges for trying to rob her blind, then that girl would be in jail where she belongs."

"Billy?" Dom asked, loosening his tie. Swanson in his first incarnation?

"Billy Wright, the no-account boy she used to hang around with. He put his mother in the hospital and walked away scot-free. The pair of them was always trouble. But they're like greased pigs. Nobody can catch 'em."

They certainly had to have a layer of Teflon to work scams this long without another arrest. And his gut started vibrating like mad at the mention of the incident with Wright's mother. He'd have to look into it. "Do you have any idea where I can find this Billy Wright? Maybe he knows where I could find Ms. Pedley."

"Pah! He hasn't set foot in Brevard County since he left town with Davina."

"When was that?"

"Twelve, no thirteen years ago. Good riddance, I say. You're better off keeping the money, son."

"I'm afraid the law won't allow me."

Mrs. Mullins released a big sigh. "She never gave two hoots about the law, but it's nice to know some people still do."

As he spoke, Dom spread out Swanson's case file on the kitchen table. "What about Mr. Wright's mother? Is she still around?"

"Not that it's going to do you any good. That woman ain't been right in the head since the accident."

"She's still in the hospital?"

"Doubt it. It's been ten years."

Dom rubbed the heel of one hand on his temple. "Do you know where she is?"

"Umph, we weren't that close," she said and made it sound as if garbage was more fragrant than an association with the Wrights.

"Because of her son?" Dom asked.

"We're a respectable community here. People like the Pedleys and the Wrights just didn't fit in."

"Why's that?"

"Loose morals," Mrs. Mullins whispered, as if the neighbors could hear her.

"Did Ms. Pedley have any other friends in the neighborhood?"

"The girl was a loner. Maybe if she'd had friends, she wouldn't have turned to crime to get away from home. Maude tried to help her out and look how she got paid back."

Mrs. Mullins seemed more than willing to gossip, so Dom kept the questions coming. The picture the old woman painted wasn't a pretty one. Neglect and abuse had stamped both Davina Pedley's and Billy Wright's childhoods. With a neighborhood standing in judgment, it was no wonder they'd turned to each other. The question was, who was leading whom?

Chapter Thirteen

Red, orange and yellow stripes invited patrons in and led them inside the fitness center. The main room held a variety of treadmills, elliptical machines, bikes, steppers and Cybex machines facing four television screens set to various stations. At the back, a mirror-lined exercise room for classes was set off for privacy, along with what looked like a couple of offices. Through the exercise room's window, Luci spotted Amber teaching a class. Tinny flute music emanated from speakers. Luci made her way across the empty exercise floor.

Amber was leading the five students in the class through a final stretching pose. In spite of the gray one-piece yoga suit that sapped the color from her skin, the glow of sweat added a certain kind of beauty to Amber's doll features.

An interview was a conversation with purpose, and Luci's nerves fired wildly at the thought of getting something out of this one. Dom was the talking head. Not her. She'd almost flunked the negotiation portion of the training. Dom had aced it. What if she blew it? What if she got nothing usable out of Amber and it made things worse for Jill?

Luci pasted on a smile and waved at Amber. Amber dismissed the class, then said, "Give me a minute and I'll meet you in my office." She pointed to the second closed door and headed toward what Luci assumed must be the ladies' room.

"Okay. Take your time." Luci stepped into Amber's office and adjusted the camera inside the starburst pin on her sweater and her loose hair over the earpiece Dom had fitted her with.

"I'm in Amber's office. Can you hear me?" she whispered.

"Loud and clear." Dom's smooth voice buffed the edge off her raw nerves.

She took in Amber's space. "Everything's neat and tidy."

"You're going to do just fine," Dom's voice spoke into her ear like a caress. "Just relax."

He breathed with her and she found her muscles loosening their tension.

A poster with a tropical island scene graced the back wall of Amber's office. Otherwise nothing cheered the dreary room. No window, just an overhead fluorescent fixture that buzzed and clicked. The computer screen was black. The calendar—an exercise company give-away—on the corkboard had rectangles of classes blocked out in black pen. Amber's agenda, opened to today's date, showed several appointments with clients. Luci quickly flipped back through the pages and noticed several lunch dates with Jill, but nothing with Warren or any other man. All of the phone numbers in the tele-phone directory section were local. She brought the camera pin close. "Can you see the numbers?"

"Hold it steady."

Footsteps approached on the industrial gray carpet. "She's coming."

Luci retreated to the guest chair in front of the desk and pretended to be engrossed in the soft music tinkling through the speakers. "What's playing? It's so soothing."

"An instrumental mix. I'm not sure exactly who the group is."

"It's very nice. You looked as if you were really enjoying your class. What was it?"

"Pilates."

"Made me want to join in."

"Pilates strengthens and conditions core muscles and improves flexibility and joint mobility." Amber opened a drawer and retrieved a brochure, as well as a pale blue sheet outlining payment options. "Here. We're always looking for new members. We have beginner classes as well as more advanced ones."

Luci feigned interest in the brochure. "Have you been doing this for long?"

Amber shrugged. "A while. I'm a certified instructor, if that's your worry."

Dom's voice wafted seemingly right into her brain. "That's it. Build rapport."

"No, I was just thinking that you're lucky to have found a job that feels like play," Luci said. "Jill said you took over running the center from Dana Booth when she left on maternity leave."

Amber gave a small smile. "Yes, a fortunate opening for me."

"Is that what you did before you moved to New Hampshire?"

"I've always had an interest in fitness."

Luci stuffed the brochure in her purse. "How people land where they live fascinates me. Did family bring you here?"

"I came for a vacation and liked it so much, I decided to stay." Amber plopped her forearms on the blotter. "So, do you have any ideas for Jill's shower?"

Luci dragged her chair closer to the desk and leaned forward conspiratorially. "Actually, I was wondering if we could talk about Warren first."

Amber blinked her surprise. "Warren, what for?"

"Well, you introduced him to Jill, so I thought you might know a bit more about him."

Amber sank back in her chair. "I don't know him all that well."

"Mirror her," Dom reminded Luci.

Luci leaned back. "But well enough to introduce him to Jill."

Amber shrugged one shoulder. "We just ran into him at the club, that's all."

"Do you know him from his work?"

Amber bit onto the offered explanation just a bit too fast. "I had him do a search for a client who skipped out without paying her bill."

"Oh." Luci played the disappointed card for all it was worth. "What do you think about him?"

The pale pink of Amber's manicured nails skated up and down the sides of her black leather agenda. "He seems nice enough."

"That's just it." Luci infused her voice with puzzlement. "There's so much mystery about him. None of his friends or family is coming to the wedding. My mother's so disappointed."

Amber straightened her back and crossed her legs, giving off an aura as elegant as a finishing school graduate. "Well, the state wouldn't have given him a private detective's license if he didn't pass the background check, so he has to be all right. He found my missing client and the center got paid."

"Still, you'd think he'd want someone there for his big day."

Amber tilted her head. "Maybe he doesn't have anyone. It's not everybody who has a nice family like yours."

"Oh, I hadn't thought of that." Luci leaned forward and lowered her voice. "Do you think he comes from a troubled background?"

"Well, if he did, he's overcome it."

"She's shutting down," Dom said. "Move on to the statement script."

"The thing is, Amber, I haven't trusted Warren from the second I heard about him. And nothing you've said has changed my mind about him. I know he's going to hurt Jill and your answers make me think you know he is and that you're helping him." Luci paused, waiting for Amber's reaction. It came swiftly and vehemently.

"Why would Warren want to hurt your sister?"

"I know what he's going to do."

Amber's pale pink nails trailed down her throat. "As far as I know, he has no reason to want to hurt Jill."

"He steals money, Amber. He breaks hearts. Why would you think that he wouldn't hurt anyone?"

Amber snapped the agenda shut as if she could close

the conversation just as easily. "I have no idea what you're talking about."

"Of course you do, because you're helping him. You're the one who handles the fund transfers that cleans out the victims." Luci leaned closer into Amber's personal space. "Did you know he killed Laynie McDaniels and Carissa Esslinger?"

Her eyes widened. "He wouldn't kill anyone."

"So you were the one who killed them?"

Amber stood, arms soldier-stiff and still at her side. "I have no idea what you're talking about. I think you should leave now."

"Show her you believe she's a good person," Dom said.

"Tell me the truth," Luci said, standing as straight as Amber, then softened her stance just a bit. "Me, I'm not anyone, except Jill's sister. Nothing you tell me can be used against you. The cops won't be as nice. I know what Warren's done. I know you're helping him. What I can't understand is why you would want to. You seem like such a nice person. The way you're running the fitness center, you seem to have such potential to serve the community. Why would you help Warren scam innocent women out of their life's savings?"

"Innocent women?" Her brown eyes slitted and her mouth pinched.

"I don't see a bad person in front of me. I'm thinking that he has to have something on you to gain your cooperation that way."

"Of course not. I haven't done anything wrong."

Luci put a finger to her lower lip. "Not even when you tried to scam a little old lady when you were eighteen?"

Amber's fingertips went white against the desktop. "That was wrong of me and I gave every cent back. That was a long time ago and it has nothing to do with my life today."

"Play up the cognitive distortion," Dom coached in her ear.

"I'm thinking that you must have been desperate to steal from the employer who trusted you," Luci said pensively. "Was she so old that she sometimes forgot to pay you? Sometimes it's hard for old people to remember what they've done. And with your mother drunk so much of the time, you probably needed money just to survive."

"What do you know about my life?" Amber scoffed.

Luci noticed that Amber was no longer denying her allegations. "I know you had it rough. I know that you made a wrong decision, but that you were smart enough to realize you'd acted wrong and returned what you took." She made a show of looking around her. "And I know you can do good, if you want to."

"You don't know anything."

Luci tilted her head. "Then make me understand."

"There's nothing to understand. Whatever you think I've done, I swear to God I didn't do it."

"I just want to protect Jill," Luci said. "She has a young son who depends on her—just like you wanted to depend on your mother, but couldn't because she was drunk."

Amber gasped. "I want you to leave now."

"Minimize her culpability," Dom whispered.

"I can't hurt you," Luci pressed. "But if you're not going to help me, you're not going to leave me any choice but to turn over all I have to the police. You haven't done anything wrong yet, but if you keep protecting Warren, then you're going to become an accessory. You'll go to jail. But if you help me catch Warren, then there's no crime on your part."

Amber rose from her chair, tracked to the door and opened it. "We're done talking."

Her face was set in a you-can't-make-me-talk-no-matter-what-you-pull manner. All color seemed to wash out of her skin, leaving it a pasty white. She licked her lips repeatedly as if their dryness was painful.

Law enforcement rarely dealt with people who wanted to tell the truth. People lied in two ways—by commission or by omission, meaning they told whoppers or danced around the truth. But deceit of either kind left clues. Amber's vague answers, her swearing to God, her paling face and drying mouth all but secreted the scent of stress. They'd hit a nerve, but Amber was holding firm.

"Yank her chain and see what happens," Dom said.

"I have proof that Warren is pulling a sweetheart scam," Luci said. "I have proof that he's changed his identity at least five times. I have proof that he killed two women."

Amber shook her head. "He didn't kill anyone. That's just not like him."

Luci moved to the door and swiveled so that Amber couldn't escape. "I have proof that he's going to pull the same scam on Jill and that you were the one to set up the meet. Now I've seen Warren in action. I know he can be quite charming. He's the type of person that's really hard to say no to. But he's using you, Davina. And you don't want to be the one taking the fall for what he's done."

"Which is nothing." Her voice was low and harsh. "If you had the proof you say you have, you wouldn't be here harassing me."

"Show her the file," Dom said.

Luci pulled out the photographs of Warren with his victims from the case file in her bag. She fanned them out as if they were playing cards and waved them in front of Amber's face.

"That doesn't mean anything," Amber insisted.

Luci shrugged and stuffed the photographs back in the file, making sure Amber could see the fullness of their investigation. "You deserve better than the way Warren is treating you."

"Warren cares about me."

"He's sleeping with another woman." Luci tilted her head. "What does it mean when a man says he loves you, but sleeps with another woman?"

Amber frowned. "He's not sleeping with them."

"You can't be that naive."

"He's *not* sleeping with them."

"Jill says the sex is good." Luci returned the file to her purse. "When a man disappears from your life for months at time, when he courts another woman, sleeps with that woman, marries that woman, he has no feelings toward the woman he's cheating on."

Amber cranked her chin up. "It's not cheating if I know about it."

"When a man refuses to talk to a woman in public, refuses to touch her when anyone else is watching, refuses to acknowledge she exists, he has no feelings for her."

Amber opened her mouth.

"When a man loves a woman," Luci interrupted, a sudden restlessness squirming through her stomach, "he treats her like a queen. He makes her feel good. He lets her know he wants to be around her, with her. He keeps his word. He's there for her."

Luci's stomach plummeted to her feet. Oh, God, Dom loved her. He really loved her. She cleared her throat.

"I saw you talking to Warren at the carnival. That's not the right way to treat a woman, Davina. You're pretty. You have brains. Why would you accept to be treated like garbage?"

Amber crossed her arms under her chest. "It's not like that. It's a business transaction."

Interesting choice of words. "He's actually got you believing that?"

Amber sighed wearily. "You have it all wrong. We have a dream. We're going to get a boat and sail the world."

"Is that your dream, Davina, or his?"

Amber glanced at the tropical island poster. "*Ours.* It's our dream."

"Use Swanson's real name," Dom said. "See if she uses it, too."

"Then why hasn't Billy made it happen already?" Luci asked. "Why is he dragging you year after year into a life of crime?"

"We have to wait until his mother's dead because, you know, we don't want to leave her alone." Amber shook her head. "Billy, he thinks it's his fault his mother's the way she is."

"You've got her," Dom said, excitement filling his voice.

"Why would he think that?" Luci asked.

"It *was* an accident."

"What was an accident?"

"Her falling down the stairs."

"When was this?"

"A long time ago." Amber dismissed her comment with a careless wave of her hand. "When we were in high school."

"What happened?"

"The guy Billy's mother was dating was a jerk. Billy knew that, but he still left her alone with him. He didn't want to miss the senior trip. He'd paid for it himself and he wanted to go. When he got home that night, he found his mother unconscious at the bottom of the stairs."

Somehow, Luci doubted this was the real unfolding of events that night. Would they ever know the truth? "Alive?"

"Well, of course, or she wouldn't be in the nursing home now, would she?"

"You tell me. Is she still in the nursing home?"

"Last time I checked."

"Which was?"

"A week ago."

"Is she lucid?"

"His mother?" Amber shook her head. "She's awake, but something's wrong with her brain. She just kinda stares right through a body, you know. Billy's always hoping she'll remember him, but she never does. She doesn't remember much of anything."

"Maybe she doesn't want to remember the person

who hurt her." Luci took a step toward Amber. "You still have a chance, Davina. Talk to me. Tell me the truth about Billy. Why is he deliberately seeking out women like my sister?"

"You've got him all wrong."

"He's using you, Davina."

"He's taking care of me."

Warren had Amber so snowed she couldn't see the truth staring her in the face.

"I'm not going to let Billy hurt Jill," Luci said. "We're watching Jill's accounts. The second he moves a penny out of any of them, the police are going to come down on him. Unless you help us, you're going down with him. You have twenty-four hours to think about it." Luci stepped out the door. "I'll be waiting to hear from you."

"WHAT DO YOU think?" Luci asked him as she settled into the cab of his truck.

Dom helped Luci remove the camera pin and earpiece. "I think Amber's one tough cookie and we're going to need a sledgehammer to break her."

A sad look crossed Luci's green eyes. "She's not going to give Warren up. What do you suppose he has on her?"

Dom couldn't help himself, he let his fingers linger on Luci's loose hair. "Or her on him. She's holding on pretty tightly. If she's the mastermind, she has as much to lose as Warren."

"So what next?"

Next, he wanted to box Luci safely and keep her out of harm's way. Once Swanson found out Luci had made him, things were going to move fast and he didn't want her in the way. "You're going to go about your regularly scheduled life. And I'm going to shadow our little friend here for a while."

"You think she'll go running to Warren?"

"No doubt."

Luci frowned. "What about Warren?"

"His car's still parked at his office and we have someone tailing him."

Luci sighed. "Watch and wait."

"That's the main course of our profession."

THE CALL CAME just as Warren was contemplating going to Jill's.

"You have to get out," Amber said, her voice thick with anxiety.

"I told you never to call me here."

"She's on to you. Jill's sister. She knows about the other women."

"Why'd you have to open your big fat trap?" Warren jabbed the computer mouse, clicking off the photo of the boat waiting for him in Miami.

"I didn't say a word. She tried to make me talk about what you've done, but I didn't tell her anything."

"Then I don't have anything to worry about." He shut down the computer.

"She knows about your mother. She thinks you killed Laynie McDaniels and Carissa Esslinger."

"You know that's not true." As far as everyone was concerned, those women had killed themselves. They shouldn't have come after him. They should have stayed home and learned their lessons.

"That's what I told her," Amber said, the whine in her voice as irritating as a mosquito's. "But she's gunning for you, Billy. She's not going to let you touch her sister's money. She says Jill's accounts are being watched. That the second you try to take any money, the cops are going to nail you."

Warren got up and wandered over to the window. The dark sedan was still parked across the street. How much of this conversation were the electronic ears pointed in his direction capturing? He liked to win, but he wasn't a fool. There were plenty more sinners waiting for a lesson. He should have cut his losses the minute he'd met the sister and tagged her as trouble. But the million-dollar payday was hard to give up. Still, there was time enough to make his mark on Jill. She couldn't get away without realizing the weight of her sins. "Here's what I want you to do. I want you to meet me at Jill's. How long will it take you to get here?"

"Fifteen, twenty minutes. I have to close the fitness center."

"Make it half an hour. I want to pick up some groceries first."

"Groceries?"

He hung up without answering her pesky questions. The less she knew, the better for him. He slipped on his suit jacket and closed up the office as if it were just another day. Making a great show of leaving, he headed for his car. As he pulled out of the parking lot and onto Main Street, he picked up his tail.

At the grocery store, he found a slot near the entrance. Inside, he made sure to walk in front of the window to pick up a cart. As soon as he was out of viewing range, he dumped the cart and headed toward the back entrance.

As he'd expected, the sedan was parked at the far end of the lot near a Dumpster. The private dick's binoculars were trained at the exit. That got 'em every time. Warren carefully made his way around the back of the car. With the safety hammer in his right hand, he broke the glass on the driver's side. With his left hand, he ran a blade across the surprised dick's throat.

Chapter Fourteen

When Jill returned with the boys from soccer practice, Warren was waiting for her in the living room. The setting sun spread a perfect red glow across the white carpet. Shedding shoes, balls and bags as they went, the boys raced straight up the stairs to Jeff's room—as he knew they would. Their routine was second nature by now. He'd counted on it and was rewarded for his forbearance.

Jill flitted into the kitchen and paused at the counter to drop her purse. "Warren? What are you doing here so early?"

"I came to visit you, my heart." Reluctantly he rose from the rich comfort of the leather couch. "Is that a crime?"

Her smile bloomed all the way to her eyes. God, she was easy. She turned on the kitchen light, sashayed to him and wrapped her arms around his neck. "You can visit me any time."

He clamped his hands around her hips and dropped his forehead against hers. "Here's what's going to happen. You're going to follow my instructions to the letter and everything will be all right."

"What? Warren?" Wrinkles grooved her forehead.

He pulled a Beretta from his jacket pocket and placed the cold metal against her cheek. "Call the boys."

She sucked in a sharp breath and tried to pull back. "Warren? What's going on? I don't understand."

His hand held her in place in a viselike grip that would leave bruises. "You're too stupid to understand. I said call the boys now."

She shook her head in confusion. "But—"

"Now," he growled between clenched teeth.

She gulped. Her frightened eyes never left his. "Jeff! Brendan! Come down here for a minute."

"Aww, Mom! We're in the middle of a game!"

"Come down, please. It's important."

Warren smiled his approval. "When they get here, you'll tie them up with this duct tape, and you'll put them in the closet. Is that understood?"

"Warren, you're scaring me. Why are you doing this? What's wrong?"

"Shut up! If you want things to turn out right for you and your boy, then you're going to shut up and listen."

"Warren—"

He poked the muzzle of the pistol against her temple. Her gulp of fear made him hard. He shoved the roll of duct tape into her hand as the boys trampled down the stairs like a herd of buffalo and spilled into the living room, laughing. He stuck the Beretta in his jacket pocket, but made sure Jill saw he had it pointed in the boys' direction. His mouth brushed the shell of her ear. "Which one first, Jilly? Your son or Luci's?"

"Warren, please."

"Mommy, what's wrong?" Jeff said, his eyes as big

as a fish's behind the lenses of his glasses. It should be against the law to make a kid look that geeky. Those glasses were a target to bullies. Pick on me. She might as well have painted a bull's-eye on the boy's forehead. *I'm saving you, kid. Your mother's never going to let herself fall for another man after me. You'll be her whole life. Just like you deserve.*

Jill's eyes pleaded. Her mouth trembled. "Warren, please, don't do this. I love you."

No, she loved the idea of being loved, of being taken care of. She didn't even know who he was, hadn't even tried to find out. Ruthlessly, he pressed the pistol in his pocket so she would make out its clear outline. "Which one?"

"Come here, boys." Jill crouched and called to them with both palms up. She tried to keep a stoic face, but she wasn't a very good actress and tears dripped down her cheeks. As the boys got close enough, she hauled them into her shaking arms. Too little, too late. He wasn't going to fall for her false pang of motherhood.

"We're going to play a little game, okay," Jill said. The brave smile she put on for the boys wavered.

"I don't want to, Mommy."

"Do as your mother says," Warren ordered.

"It's a game called 'Capture,'" Jill said, squeezing both boys. "I tie you up and hide you, then Auntie Luci will try to find you when she gets here."

"Doesn't sound like a fun game," Brendan said, eyebrows scrunched down low over his eyes. He looked as stubborn as his mother. He'd be the first one to go if things got tight.

"You don't have a choice, kid," Warren said. "Now stick out your arms."

"Mommy?" Jeff reached his arms up and wound them around his mother's neck.

Brendan tried to run, but Warren stopped him with a grip on the shoulders.

"It's okay, Jeff." At least Jill had the sense to know when to obey. She unwound her son's arms from around her neck, ripped a piece of duct tape from the roll and looped it around his thin wrists.

Jeff started bawling. "I don't like this game, Mommy."

Brendan kicked at Warren's leg, hitting him square on the shin. The blow reverberated down to the bone. "You're a bad man!"

Warren picked up the little monster by the scruff of sweatshirt and lifted him off the ground. It's kids like this one that had made his school years hell.

Jill sprang up and reached for the boy. "No, please, leave him alone. Brendan, honey, you have to let me tie you up."

"No! I want to go home. My mom won't like this."

With surprising strength, Jill pried Brendan from Warren's grip. "It's just a game, honey. Your mom's going to be here soon and she'll find you. Okay?"

"Just tie him up!" But Jill was right. Luci, the troublemaker, was going to show up to pick up her son at any minute. He had to be ready to handle her, too.

Jill awkwardly bound Brendan's wrists and ankles with duct tape. Was she going to take all day? Warren barked, "Open the pantry!"

Pointing his Beretta at Jeff, he hefted Brendan by the waist of his pants.

Jill obeyed meekly and opened the kitchen pantry.

"Aren't things easier when you just pay attention to the right things?" Warren said and shoved Brendan into the pantry. "Bring the other one."

"Warren, I don't understand why you're doing this."

"Bring the other one."

Hugging her son close, she gently set him down in the pantry. "You just sit here and we'll finish the game soon." After a final kiss, she clicked on the overhead light and shut the door.

Weapon pointed at Jill, Warren grabbed a kitchen chair and shoved it under the doorknob.

The front door opened. "Jill? Warren?"

"Amber, run!" Jill shouted. "He's got a gun. Get help."

Amber appeared at the kitchen opening. "Warren?"

"Amber, run!"

"I thought—" Amber started.

Just what he didn't need, another woman attempting to think. "It's about time you got here."

"I waited like you said."

"Amber?" Jill's face collapsed and both her hands reached for her heart as if it were breaking on the spot. God, he loved it when realization finally hit. What a treat it was to watch it firsthand.

"Don't look so surprised, Jill," Warren said, opening one arm to Amber. Obediently, Amber filled the space. He bent his head and planted an openmouthed kiss on her lips while he kept the Beretta pointed at Jill.

"Amber?" The truth seemed to dawn on Jill, twisting her pretty face into a mask of horror. "Amber? What's going on?"

"Jill, meet my wife, Davina Wright."

Jill's gaze bounced from one to the other, limbs shaking as if winter had struck early and fast. "Your wife? What are you saying?"

"I'm saying that your sister was right. You've been duped. And you made it so easy, too." He released Amber. "You can thank your sister for your position right now. If she'd let things alone, in two weeks, you'd have been a free woman, cleansed of your sins."

"Cleansed?"

"For being a selfish bitch more interested in finding a man than raising your son." Warren crowded her, caressed her cheek with the barrel of the pistol and whispered in her ear the words that would bring her salvation. "Understand this. You're going to go to the bank. You're going to withdraw everything in your accounts—all three of them. You're going to bring me the cash. And then, if everything goes well, I'm going to leave, and you'll never see me again."

"But—"

"You're not listening to me, Jill. You have no choice here. If you call the police, if you try to call your sister, if you so much as hint to the teller that all is not perfectly well, then I will kill your son and your sister's son. Do you understand?"

Mute, for once, Jill nodded.

"Good," Warren said. "Just to be sure you'll be a good girl, I'm going to send Amber with you. Two friends, out running errands together."

Warren strode to the kitchen and picked up Jill's purse from the counter. He pitched the leather bag at her. She caught it with an oomph. "Go! Now! You've got an hour, then I shoot one of the boys. Which one, Jill? Jeff or Brendan?" He lifted her chin with the muzzle of the pistol and smiled at her. "Tell you what, I'll make it a surprise." He glanced down at his watch. "Your time starts now."

A BAD FEELING COILED into Dom's gut as he followed Amber down the country club road and watched her pull into Jill's driveway. If Amber was going to Jill's house to warn Swanson, then Jill could be in danger. The car in Jill's driveway wasn't Swanson's, but the lead in his stomach told him Swanson was in the house. Dom parked around the curve so his truck wouldn't be visible from Jill's house. He took his weapon from the glove compartment, checked the holster that carried his backup weapon around his ankle and made his way to the back yard.

Through the tall windows, the scene he saw made his blood turn cold. Warren had a weapon trained at Jill's head. Amber was doing nothing to help Jill. Where were the boys?

Dom pressed himself against the shake-shingle siding and put in a call to Seekers. "I've got a situation."

"Where are you?" Kingsley asked.

"Jill Courville's house." Dom gave the address and a synopsis of the situation.

"I'll alert the area SWAT team. Falconer's on his way."

"Appreciate it."

Just when he thought the situation couldn't get worse, the sound of Luci's van turning in the driveway stopped his heart, then sent it tearing at full speed. He dialed her cell phone, but she didn't pick up.

Before he could move, she entered the house. Swanson spun Jill into his arm, snubbed the muzzle of his weapon against her temple and left Luci no choice but to compliantly do his bidding.

"HE'S USING YOU, Amber," Luci said as she sat in the love seat, facing Warren holding her sister prisoner by the neck. Every nerve in Luci's body was on fire and pulsing. *Don't look at Jill's horror-stricken face.* This wasn't happening. This couldn't be happening. It was a nightmare come to life.

"Shut up!" Warren's spittle flew like a sweating bull's.

"If he pulls that trigger," Luci continued, forcing herself to focus on Amber, "you're looking at murder." Warren wouldn't fire at Jill. He'd shoot at the source of his pain—which would be her. "Do you really think he's going to protect you?"

"Don't listen to her," Warren said in a bored voice. "Tie her up. Now!"

Amber picked up the purse Jill had dropped and shoved it on the counter. She grabbed the roll of duct tape and came at Luci. "He won't let me go to jail. He's saved me before."

"He can't talk his way out of murder the way he could a simple scam."

"Tape her mouth," Warren said. "Then we won't have to listen to any more of her garbage."

"He's going to leave you here, Amber. It's getting too hot. That dream boat you talked about? He's bought it and it's in his name only. Yours is nowhere on the paperwork."

"He doesn't have a boat." Amber wound the tape around Luci's wrists. All the Pilates toning and conditioning was paying off. The little witch had one tight grip.

Luci squeezed as much space as she could between her wrists. "Ask Jill. He bought it a few days ago. A nice forty-footer."

Amber's glance darted to Warren and Jill. Eyes wide and throat working overtime, Jill nodded. "I paid for it myself. He was going to teach me to sail."

"It's so you won't be connected to me, Davina," Warren practically purred. "That's how we always work it."

Luci spread her ankles as far apart as she could as Amber wrapped tape around her legs. "Except this time, he's planning on letting you take the fall by yourself. Someone's going to have to pay and it's not going to be him."

"Hurry up with that tape!" Warren's voice rumbled with impatience. Luci gulped as the muzzle of his weapon jiggled restlessly against Jill's temple. Jill was putting on a brave front, but even from across the room, Luci could tell she was shaking.

"Whose handiwork is going to show up when all the money transfers are sorted out? Yours, Davina. Your computers. Your IDs. Your bank accounts."

Amber's fingers fumbled, so she used her teeth to cut a strip of tape. She slapped it at Luci's mouth and missed.

"Who provided the fake IDs, Davina? You did. Why do you think he let you do all the dirty work?"

Amber came at her again, teeth bared.

"He set you up to take the fall, Davina. Just like he did all the other women he scammed."

Warren shifted his weapon from Jill's head to her. His finger squeezed the trigger. Jill screamed and threw herself against the gun hand.

"No!" Luci tried to scream through the tape and lunged up toward her sister. Her heart thundered in her ears. Everything slowed. Her tied body started falling forward across Amber. Jill's scream echoed and reechoed against the living room's high ceiling. The gun fired. Glass from the tall window behind Luci exploded. Warren threw Jill out of his grasp. Blood spread across her face, her hair and dripped onto the white carpet. Her body bounced on the floor, then lay still.

Luci, taking Amber with her, crashed onto the table. Luci used the momentum to reel herself and Amber sideways onto the carpet. Amber's head hit the wooden edge of the celadon chair with a *thunk*. Her breath whooshed out. Luci continued to roll off of Amber, then strained toward the spot where her sister lay.

Jill! Jill! Jill!

But Jill didn't move.

"PUT THE GUN down!" Dom kneeled at the broken window, weapon trained toward Swanson.

"I don't think so." Swanson squeezed off two quick shots.

Dom dove for cover behind the wall. Adrenaline pumped through his veins, kicking his heart into high gear, narrowing his field of vision. He slid his back up the wall and peered into the house. Swanson was in the pantry, using the boys as a human shield. His left arm was looped around Jeff. His right arm circled Brendan, the muzzle of the gun pressed into the underside of Brendan's jaw. The boys' tears tore at him.

Where the hell was SWAT?

"Warren, this is Dom," he said calmly, trying to block out the fact that Swanson was holding a gun to Cole's son's head, that Jill was still and pale, blood pooling around her head, that Luci was lying in the middle of the living room making a perfect target. He swallowed hard. He didn't have any choice. He'd have to talk Swanson down until he could get a clear shot or backup arrived. "What's going on?"

"Dom, help!" Brendan cried, his voice rippling with fear.

"Shut up, you brat!" Swanson jabbed the muzzle deeper into Brendan's flesh, sending a jolt of adrenaline down Dom's spine.

Dom crouched closer to the window opening. Holding Swanson in his sight, he used his peripheral vision to check on Amber and Luci. Amber lay unconscious for now. Luci's green eyes burned with a potent mix of anger, fear and grit against her too pale skin. "Warren, I heard a shot a few minutes ago. How's everybody doing in there?"

"Everyone's fine. And if you want it to stay that way, you need to leave."

"Warren, what's going on?"

"What does it look like?" Sarcasm oozed from Warren's voice.

"Looks like something's spooked you and you're trying to find a way out." Dom checked his watch. Five minutes had passed since he'd called Seekers. What was taking the SWAT team so long?

"Damn right."

"Let's talk this out."

"It's too late for that."

Dom tuned into the anxiety creeping into Swanson's voice. Hostage takers were most likely to hurt someone when they were under stress. "We've got plenty of time, Warren. We're in no rush."

"Like you said, I'm in a corner."

"Well, we can move that corner. As long as everyone's okay, then there's time to make something happen."

"All the time in the world isn't going to change anything." Strain fractured Swanson's voice.

"We can work something out. Let's talk it out."

"You have no authority."

"No, but that's what makes it great. As long as you show me some good faith and release the kids, I can let you walk out of here and you can disappear. All I care about is getting everybody out safely."

Swanson barked a mirthless laugh. "I'm going to die anyway."

"What makes you say that?"

"You won't let me walk away."

"That's Hollywood. Real life doesn't work like that. The cops would rather see you walk out with your own power than have to go in there to get you. But I haven't called the cops yet. This is just between you and me. Come on, Warren, show me some good faith here. Send the boys out and I'll throw you my phone. That way you'll know I can't talk to anyone."

Dom couldn't quite make out Warren's mumbling, but the next thing he knew, Jeff was stumbling toward him. Dom urged the boy toward him with his hand and caught him as he nearly fell out of the broken window. He ripped the tape between Jeff's wrists.

"Do you see that house?" Dom pointed to the nearest neighbor away from the confrontation.

Crying, Jeff nodded.

"I want you to run there as fast as you can. Okay?" Dom said so only Jeff would hear. "Tell them to call the police. Tell them your mom is hurt and she needs an ambulance."

"I want my mommy."

"Shh. I know. I'm going to get her out. Don't you worry. But right now, I need you to be really brave and get help for your mom. Can you do that?"

With a look back through the broken window at his mother's still body, Jeff nodded again.

"That's a good boy. Go on. Run to that house and stay there."

Jeff sped away on wobbly legs. Dom turned back to Swanson. "I made you a promise and I'm keeping it." He threw in his cell phone through the window. It bounced on the carpet, then skittered across the kitchen floor.

One down. But Swanson still held Brendan in his lap, his weapon under the boy's chin. Sweat soaked Dom's shirt in spite of the cold evening air swirling around him. He couldn't allow Luci to lose her son. She'd lost too much already.

"Do you need anything, Warren?" Dom asked, looking for something neutral to get Warren talking again. "Talk to me. I can't help you if I don't know what you want."

"Make sure that there's enough money to cover my mother's funeral."

Dom ground his teeth. Swanson was making a living will, telling Dom that he wanted to die. "If you want your mother taken care of, you'll have to do it yourself. Nobody's going to die here."

"You're armed."

"So are you. I'm trusting you not to shoot, just like you're trusting me. But I'm going to show you my good faith by throwing my weapon away." Swanson didn't need to know he had a backup. Dom removed the backup .22 from the holster strapped at his ankle, then pushed the Glock Warren was expecting through the hole in the window. The gun fell to the floor where Swanson could see it, but not reach it without exposing himself. He shot Luci a quick glance and hoped to God she could get to it if necessary. "It's just you and me, now, Warren. Let's figure out how we're going to get you out of here."

"Amber has the account number for the nursing home."

"You're going to need to do that yourself. My only goal is to get you out of this house and on your way. Do you have money? I've got a couple hundred in my wallet. That should last you a couple of days. Jill probably has more in her purse. I can see her purse on the counter. Why don't I have a look?"

"You're trying to trick me."

Swanson's movements were getting jerky, as if he could no longer sit still. His voice grew much louder than needed. He was talking himself into suicide-by-cop. The piece of garbage wanted to die, but was too much of a coward to do the job himself.

"I'm on your side, Warren. My truck's right outside. Here." Dom jangled the keys. "It's all yours. All you have to do is let the boy go."

Swanson was coming out in the open, his weapon pinched at Brendan's neck. "It's time to say goodbye."

"I'll trade you Brendan for the keys. You'll be across the state line in less than five minutes."

Using Brendan as a shield, Warren moved across the kitchen toward Jill's purse on the counter.

"Take the wallet out of the purse," Warren ordered Brendan.

Hands still tied in front of him, Brendan reluctantly obeyed.

Greasy eels of dread squirmed through Dom's gut. Would Swanson take the keys and run? "Here's my wallet." Dom tossed the leather billfold so it landed on the floor away from the counter. Swanson would have to bend down to pick it up or order Brendan to pick it up. Either way, Dom prayed for a clear shot. Where was the local SWAT team? Where was Falconer?

Then out of the corner of his eye, Dom saw Luci stretch her tied hands toward his discarded weapon. Fiery determination burned in her pupils.

Dom had one chance to hold Swanson long enough in one spot for Luci to take a shot. He tucked the backup .22 in the waist of his jeans and rose. He held out his keys, pulse pounding like before the first kickoff of a football season, when the whole game waited on one whistle. "I've given you everything you need to get away, Warren. Let the boy go."

Chapter Fifteen

Jill's body lay crumpled on the carpet. Dark red stained the white fibers. Luci couldn't reach her sister, couldn't stop the blood. She was as helpless to help Jill as she'd been to help Cole. *Jill, I'm so sorry. I tried to keep you safe.*

Luci's pulse beat out of time. Her mouth was desert-dry. Why couldn't she have let things alone? Why did she have to meddle? Hadn't she learned anything? She pushed the self-defeating thoughts out of her mind. *Jill needs medical attention now.*

Her fingers stretched toward Dom's Glock. What if she missed? What if Warren killed Brendan or Dom? *And if you do nothing, Luci, then what?* Gritting her teeth, she molded her hands against the cold grip, index on the trigger.

She took in the mask of rage darkening Warren's face. One bullet. That's all that stood between death and the people she loved.

Watch and don't blink. Be ready.

Discipline. Control. Restraint.

You can do it. You have to do it.

Please, please, please. Don't let Brendan die. Don't let Dom die. Don't let Jill die.

She already had too many souls on her conscience. Dom loved her. And she hadn't had the chance to tell him that she loved him, too. Loving was a risk, but it was worth it—even if it didn't last. Her life was richer for having loved Cole. He was dead, but he'd always be with her through Brendan. And Dom was her promise of a brighter future. She wouldn't let Warren snatch him away from her before they'd even had a chance. And she wasn't giving up Brendan. Not for anything. She'd die first.

Slowly, so as not to give away her intent, she rolled until she lay in a forward firing position.

Brendan, oh God, her baby's face was blank with fear. His mouth hung open in a silent scream. His eyes were so round, his skin so pale.

Don't you worry, baby. Mommy'll get you out safe. That's what she once did. She saved lives.

But not this way. Not with so much on the line.

Don't look at Brendan. Don't look at Dom. Focus on the target.

Cold zero—that unpracticed leap-of-faith imprint on a target when the point of aim and the point of impact aligned—was the one shot she'd have at getting the job done. The shot she'd have to live with for the rest of her life.

Backlit by the dying sun, Dom presented himself as a perfect target. Warren shifted, loosening his hold on Brendan. Brendan elbowed his captor in the privates and lunged away.

Movement behind her.

"Billy!" Amber shouted, moved.

Breathe. Hold. Squeeze.

Aim true, Luci increased pressure on the trigger. The world exploded. Her ears rang. The smell of cordite singed her nose. Warren fell, screaming and gripping his shoulder. Dom moved in and, with a quick move, disarmed Warren and knocked him out with the butt of the weapon. Before Warren could reawaken, Dom slapped on duct-tape handcuffs.

Amber pounded on Luci's back. Pain stabbed between Luci's shoulder blades as Amber dropped on her and lunged for the Glock. It discharged. Plaster rained down. Luci struggled to keep the muzzle pointed away from Dom and Brendan. Amber's fingernails ripped into the flesh of Luci's hand, drawing blood as she tried to loosen Luci's grip. Luci kicked, bucked and twisted, rolling Amber over. Using momentum, she struck Amber on the head with the full force of anger and gun grip. Dom grabbed Amber as she prepared to pounce again and trussed her up with duct tape.

The sound of squealing tires split the air as the local police arrived. Ambulance sirens followed close behind.

It was over. Dom and Brendan were still alive.

Brendan catapulted himself at her. "Mom! Mom!"

She released the weapon, ripped the tape from her mouth and scooped her bound arms over her son's head. Sobs racked her chest as she held him tight. Refusing to let go of Brendan, she looked up at Dom. "Jill?"

Dom bent over Jill. "She's still breathing." He rushed to the front door and yanked it open. "We need a gurney in here now!"

Fight, Jill. You have to survive. Jeff needs you. I need you. Luci buried her son deeper into her arms. The adrenaline that had sustained her drained from her body and she started to shake. Brendan, Jeff and Dom were all alive.

Please, she prayed, *let Jill be okay.*

Dom PACED the waiting area of the emergency room at a local hospital, watching for Luci's return. Luci's parents, each holding one of the boys, sat nearby, as anxious as he was for a further update on Jill. The elevator doors at the other end of the waiting area opened, revealing Falconer.

"How are they?" Falconer asked.

Dom ran a hand through his hair and kneaded the tension tightening his neck. "Luci's fine. Jill was lucky. The shot that hit her was just a graze. They're going to keep her overnight for observation. Luci's helping her settle in a room now, so the kids can visit. What about Swanson, or I should say Billy Wright?"

"He's still in surgery, but the doctors expect him to pull through. He'll be under guard until he can be transferred to detention."

"What about Amber—Davina?" Spotting movement near the corridor, Dom cut his gaze in that direction. Disappointment sagged through him when Luci didn't appear.

"She's in custody, singing like a canary. That's one screwed-up woman. She really believed Wright loved her and planned to take her with him after he'd earned enough money for their 'dream.'" Falconer shook his head. "He has enough money stashed away to finance several dreams."

"It was never about the boat."

"It was about payback for parental neglect," Falconer agreed. "In addition to pretending he was a 49er, Wright also passed himself off as a Deputy U.S. Marshal, a professional skier, a paratrooper, a SWAT officer, a U.S. Customs agent, a college professor, a Navy SEAL and a private investigator."

Dom whistled. "He's been at this longer than we thought."

Falconer nodded. "Posing as a federal law enforcement officer and making false statements to obtain firearms is going to get him several federal counts. He's also going to face local charges in California, Washington, Oregon and Texas to start with. Others are likely to be added, including the murder of the private detective we hired for surveillance. He was found dead behind a Dumpster in a grocery store parking lot." Shaking his head, Falconer grunted. "Would you believe Swanson thinks he's going to get out on bail?"

"Any chance that could happen?"

Falconer shook his head. "With his ability to disappear, his flight risk is too great. They'll hold him."

"That's a relief."

Falconer clapped Dom on the back. "I'll need your report as soon as you can get it to me."

Dom nodded. "Give me a day."

"You've earned it." Falconer looked over Dom's shoulder and gave one sharp nod. "Anytime Luci wants to join the team, she's welcome."

"She'd be an asset." Dom glanced at the mouth of the corridor. Pieces of hair stuck out of Luci's braid at all angles. Dried blood stained her apple-green sweater. She walked boldly, a new confidence glowing from her.

She'd never looked more beautiful. Warmth radiated from his solar plexus, mellowed him faster than any eighteen-year-old scotch. "I've got to go."

"Where to?"

Dom shoved his hands in his jean pockets, a certain trepidation dancing in his gut. After what had happened, would Luci want him anywhere near her? This time, he wasn't going to let her go without telling her what was in his heart. Filled with hope, he said, "Home."

LUCI STOOD AWAY from the crowd of family gathered around Jill's hospital bed, unsure what her reception would be. Jeff had his arms wound around Jill's neck as if he would never let go. Her father restrained Brendan's eager curiosity about Jill's bandage. Her mother glanced back at Luci and came to stand beside her.

"Thank you for saving your sister," Barbara said, her voice warbling with emotion.

"It's my fault she got hurt in the first place. I should have shown her the evidence Dom had against Warren earlier."

"No, Lucinda." Barbara grabbed Luci's upper arms and shook her gently. "Dom explained everything. You were building a solid case against Warren so he would never hurt another woman this way. Dom told me how you helped uncover critical pieces of evidence. If you hadn't shot Warren, Jill may have bled to death. You kept Warren from hurting Brendan. I never understood what drove you to join the Hostage Rescue Team, Luci. But I see now that you helped people. You shouldn't be tending goats and farming. You should be using your talent, my darling daughter."

Tears wavered in Luci's eyes. She'd waited a lifetime for her mother's approval and it had come when she'd least expected it. "Thanks, Mom. I needed to hear that." Especially now.

A cloud of Guerlain enveloped Luci as her mother hugged her. Keeping Luci in her embrace, Barbara returned to Jill's bedside. "Come on, Jeff. We need to let your mother rest. Brendan's going to spend the night with us, too. We'll have a sleepover."

At Jill's urging, Jeff reluctantly crept out of his mother's arms.

"I want to go home, too," Jill said, pushing herself off the pillow. "Jeff needs me."

"You will do no such thing, young lady," Barbara said, letting go of Luci and wrapping an arm around each boy. "Rest. Doctor's orders. Jeff will be safe with your father and I. And he'll have Brendan for company."

"But I—"

"No arguments." Barbara shepherded the boys toward the door. "We'll come back for you in the morning when you're released."

After several rounds of saying good-night, Luci closed the hospital room door behind the boys and her parents. They had needed to see that Jill was all right. Jill had put up a brave front to reassure Jeff, but pain and fatigue were taking their toll and she now sank into the pillows.

Luci and Dom had given their statements. She'd arranged for someone to clean Jill's house as soon as the scene was released. Jill didn't need to go home to blood and broken glass. She had enough heartbreak to deal with as it was.

Luci hung on to the door handle, not quite sure what to say. "I'll let you rest. Do you need anything before I go?"

"I'm fine." Jill slanted Luci a weak smile and tapped the bandage gracing her temple. "Good thing I have a hard head."

When the adrenaline died down, Jill would hate her. After she got home to her son and her house, would she ever want to see Luci again? Her sister's friendship was what had made the last six years bearable. "I'm so sorry, Jill. I never—"

"I don't want to talk about *him*," Jill said in one breath. Then with the other, "How could I have fallen for his act?"

"How could you not? He and Amber studied you for months before they swept in for their scam." Her job had shown Luci the dark side of humanity, and Cole's death had made her hypervigilant to violence. That wariness had kept her an outsider. "You have a big heart, Jill. You see the good in everyone. It's a quality I've always envied."

Jill swiped at her eyes with the back of her hand. "I was such a fool. It's going to take me a long time to get over what he did to me."

Luci rushed to her sister's side, sat on the edge of the bed and took Jill's hand in hers. "You're alive, Jill. It could've been worse. He's killed two women."

Jill gulped. "He was right, though. I'm never going to let another man that close."

"You will because if you don't, then Warren wins." Luci squeezed Jill's hand. "There are a few good men out there, Jill. And there's one for you. You're smart.

You're beautiful. And you're too full of life to give up on love."

The door opened and Dom hesitated at the entrance.

Jill leaned her head against Luci's shoulder and whispered, "You're right. There are good men out there. You'd better hang on to this one, Lucinda."

A good man. Dom was that and more. Choked up, all Luci could do was nod.

"Thank you," Jill said, looking past Luci at Dom. "I almost made the worst mistake of my life."

"I'm glad it all turned out right."

Luci looked up at Dom. She hadn't known until she heard Dom's slow Texas drawl that she'd been listening for the sound of his voice. "You rest," she told Jill. "I'll come back in the morning."

After a prolonged goodbye, Luci and Dom managed to get away. They stopped at her parents' to check on the boys, then drove in silence to the farm. In the dark yard, Dom cut the engine. Quiet filled the night.

As she came around the van, she couldn't help it. Her gaze strayed to the empty place that had once been her barn.

"I'm sorry about all this," Dom said, coming to stand next to her and staring straight ahead into the starry night. "I never meant to put you or your family in danger."

She shivered at the memory of Warren's gun pressed under Brendan's chin. "Everybody's safe."

Dom turned to look at her, a pained expression crimping the skin around his eyes. "I love you, Luci. If anything had happened to you or Brendan, I—" He swallowed hard.

She palmed his cheek, rubbing at the prickly soft stubble of his beard. "We're all fine, and Warren and Amber will pay for their crimes."

"I love you, Luci," he insisted, leaning into her palm. "I've loved you from the second you walked into that training room twelve years ago."

His admission sent her heart into a tumble. "You never said anything."

His shoulders jerked up and his frown deepened. "You wanted Cole. He made you happy. I wanted you to be happy."

Moonlight reflected off the pale blue of his eyes. In the wide pupils, she glimpsed something deep and earnest.

"I don't want to let you go," he said, and the tight hold of fear that had chased her since Cole's death started to loosen its grip.

She didn't have to handle life alone. She could be with this man who shared her memories of Cole, who could help make a picture of the man he had been for Brendan, who understood her pain, her love and her loss. Trusting her heart, she opened herself to the greatest risk of all—loving without reservation. "Tell me what you want."

His throat worked as if speaking his needs was going to somehow reveal a weakness. "I want you and Brendan and Maggie and the chickens and the goats and anything else you can throw at me." The words came out in a rush, but his gaze remained steady and true.

She slanted her head and studied his beautiful face. A face full of contradictions—sharp cheekbones, sad eyes, an easy smile. He was there for her. Had always been there for her. All she had to do was reach out and she could wake up next to him every morning, share meals with him every day, share her life with him. Pure joy lightened her heart. And she couldn't help the smile that ran away with her lips. He had no idea what he was asking for. She hooked both hands around his nape and pulled his face toward hers until their foreheads met. "This may be the most dangerous assignment you'll ever undertake, cowboy."

His big hands reached for her and molded themselves to her back like protective wings as he pressed her as close as he could. "Well, ma'am, I *am* trained to handle high-risk situations."

"That you are." With her kiss, she showed him the love filling her heart to overflowing. Then she slid her hands down his arms, twined her fingers with his and said, "I love you. Come inside with me. Stay for a while."

"How long?" he asked.

"How does forever sound?"

A wash of peace softened his features. "I can live with that."

So could she.

Epilogue

Three weeks later

Church bells pealed, echoing with joy in Wintergreen's picturesque town square. Indian summer was in full bloom, bringing a warm breeze and a piercing blue sky. Even the trees got into the celebration of Grayson Reed's and Abrielle Holbrook's wedding with their explosion of gold and red.

Sabriel Mercer stood at the church's thick arched doorway, greeting each arriving guest with a nod, wishing he was anywhere but here. He rolled his shoulder against the stiffness of the rented tux and tugged at the too-tight collar with a finger. Only for a fellow Seeker would he endure such torture.

"Cell phone," Sabriel said and shoved forward the basket with the big cranberry bow that Liv had given him for the purpose. He wasn't sure what he'd done to deserve the humiliation of this public emasculation.

"It's off," Harper said, holding the device up so Sabriel could verify his claim.

"Orders from the boss. Hand it over."

Harper glowered. "Falconer?"

"Liv."

Without another word, Harper dropped his cell phone with the dozen already in the basket. There was no point arguing with Liv. Even the newest Seeker understood that Falconer's wife always got her way.

Standing in the shadows of the entry, Sabriel scanned the crowd seated in the wooden pews. Most were strangers, people from Reed's and Abbie's hometown.

The organ overhead in the loft stopped its nasal whine, then burst with "The Wedding March." On the arm of her former WITSEC inspector, Abbie walked down the aisle. She looked beautiful in champagne silk that made her skin glow. His own wife, Anna, had done that, too, chosen an off-white dress because she'd said the pure white made her look dead and she wanted to shine on her wedding day. Reed looked as if he'd swallowed the sun as he watched his bride make her way up the crimson carpet. Kingsley, Seeker's computer wiz, was at his side, red suspenders visible under the black tux jacket. Falconer and Liv stood arm in arm, beaming at the bride.

The newly engaged Skyralov held hands, fingers twined, with Luci. His other arm was looped around her son Brendan's shoulders. The cowboy had come into his own since he'd found them. There was a settled, peaceful air about Dom that had been missing before. Luci, a former Hostage Rescue Team sniper, had turned down an offer to work for Seekers, Inc. She'd decided to apply at the Marston Police Department instead. Watching Skyralov play Mr. Mom when Luci started the next round of police academy was going to be a kick.

Had he ever been that happy? Sabriel couldn't remember. He'd thought so once. But his marriage to Anna sometimes seemed like only a dream, eclipsed by the nightmare that had followed. As a Ranger, he'd trained hard and hot for insertions against terrorist targets, but nothing had prepared him for the utter destruction a father's grief could wreak. Sabriel almost hadn't survived.

A phone warbled a tinny melody. He frowned at his pocket. His? Other than the Seekers gathered in this church, only his mother and Tommy had this number.

And neither would dial it unless it was a matter of life or death.

* * * * *

LUCI'S COUNTRY APPLE TART

1 lemon
1 lb tart apples (2-3), peeled, cored and thinly sliced
1/2 cup sugar (reserve 2 tsp for crust)
1 tbsp flour
1/2 tsp ground cinnamon
1 pie crust (homemade or 1/2 of a 15 oz store-bought package)
1 tbsp butter, cut into 6 pieces

Preheat the oven to 450°F. Grate 1 tsp of lemon peel and squeeze 2 tbsps of juice from the lemon. Set aside. Toss the apples with the sugar, flour, cinnamon, lemon peel and juice.

Place the pie crust on a rimless baking sheet lightly dusted with flour. Dust a rolling pin with flour and roll the pastry to a 13-inch round. Heap the apples on the pastry, leaving a 2-inch border all around. Scatter the butter on the apples. Fold the pastry border back over the apples to make an uneven rustic edge of about 1 1/2 inches, leaving the slices in the center exposed. Sprinkle the reserved sugar on the pastry border.

Bake 12 minutes, then reduce the temperature to 425°F and bake until the apples are softened and bubbly and the pastry is golden-brown (12-15 mins longer). Serve warm. Makes 4 servings.

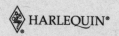

HARLEQUIN®

INTRIGUE®

The mantle of mystery beckons you to
enter the...

MISTS OF FERNHAVEN

Remote and shrouded in secrecy—our new
ECLIPSE trilogy by three of your favorite
Harlequin Intrigue authors will have you
shivering with fear and...the delightful,
sensually charged atmosphere of the
deep forest. Do you dare to enter?

WHEN TWILIGHT COMES
B.J. DANIELS
October 2005

THE EDGE OF ETERNITY
AMANDA STEVENS
November 2005

THE AMULET
JOANNA WAYNE
December 2005

eHARLEQUIN.com

The Ultimate Destination for Women's Fiction

Your favorite authors are just a click away
at www.eHarlequin.com!

- Take a sneak peek at the covers and
  read summaries of **Upcoming Books**

- Choose from over 600
  author **profiles!**

- Chat with your favorite authors
  on our **message boards.**

- Are you an author in the making?
  Get advice from published authors
  in **The Inside Scoop!**

**Learn about your favorite authors
in a fun, interactive setting—
visit www.eHarlequin.com today!**

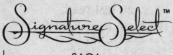

SAGA

National bestselling author

Debra Webb

**A decades-old secret threatens to bring
down Chicago's elite Colby Agency in
this brand-new, longer-length novel.**

COLBY
CONSPIRACY

While working to uncover the truth behind
a murder linked to the agency, Daniel Marks
and Emily Hastings find themselves trapped
by the dangers of desire—knowing every
move they make could be their last....

*Available in October,
wherever books
are sold.*

**Bonus Features
include:**

**Author's Journal,
Travel Tale
and
a Bonus Read.**

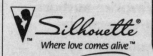

Where love comes alive™

If you enjoyed what you just read,
then we've got an offer you can't resist!

Take 2 bestselling love stories FREE!

Plus get a FREE surprise gift!

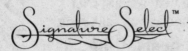

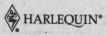

HARLEQUIN®

INTRIGUE®

As the summer comes to a close, things really begin to heat up as Harlequin Intrigue presents...

Big Sky Bounty Hunters: No man's a match for these Montana tough guys...but a woman's another story.

Don't miss this brand-new series from some of your favorite authors!

GOING TO EXTREMES
BY AMANDA STEVENS
August 2005

BULLSEYE
BY JESSICA ANDERSEN
September 2005

WARRIOR SPIRIT
BY CASSIE MILES
October 2005

FORBIDDEN CAPTOR
BY JULIE MILLER
November 2005

RILEY'S RETRIBUTION
BY RUTH GLICK,
writing as Rebecca York
December 2005

Available at your favorite retail outlet.

www.eHarlequin.com

HIBSBH

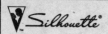

INTIMATE MOMENTS™

From *New York Times* bestselling author

Sharon Sala

comes

RIDER ON FIRE

SILHOUETTE INTIMATE MOMENTS #1387

With a hit man hot on her trail,
undercover DEA agent Sonora Jordan
decided to lie low—until ex Army Ranger
and local medicine man Adam Two Eagles
convinced her to look for the father she'd
never known...and offered her a love she'd
never known she wanted.

Available at your favorite retail outlet October 2005.

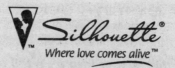

Where love comes alive™